T0356560

# THE NIGHT TREMBLES

# THE NIGHT TREMBLES

*a novel*

Nadia Terranova

Translated by
**Ann Goldstein**

SEVEN STORIES PRESS
New York / Oakland

Seven Stories Press
140 Watts Street
New York, NY 10013
www.sevenstories.com

Library of Congress Cataloging-in-Publication Data

Names: Terranova, Nadia, author. | Goldstein, Ann, 1949- translator.
Title: The night trembles : a novel / Nadia Terranova ; translated by Ann
    Goldstein.
Other titles: Trema la notte. English
Description: New York : Seven Stories Press, 2025.
Identifiers: LCCN 2024040175 | ISBN 9781644214091 (hardcover) | ISBN
    9781644214107 (ebook)
Subjects: LCGFT: Novels.
Classification: LCC PQ4920.E767 T7413 2025 | DDC 853/.92--dc23/eng/20240911
LC record available at https://lccn.loc.gov/2024040175

College professors and high school and middle school teachers may order free examination
copies of Seven Stories Press titles. Visit https://www.sevenstories.com/pg/resources-academ-
ics or email academic@sevenstories.com.

Printed in the United States of America

9  8  7  6  5  4  3  2  1

**Here where history is almost destroyed, poetry remains.**

GIOVANNI PASCOLI on the Strait of Messina and
Reggio Calabria, in *Un poeta di lingua morta*


**And Messina the siren calling**
**sad place between the Mediterranean and the stars.**

MARIETTA SALVO, "Ritornando nei luoghi," from
*Vascello fantasma*

# PRELUDE

Another moon, innocent and desperate, has risen over the Strait. It climbs above the clouds lying over the two coasts, a sickle pointing between shores that seem to touch, and there will spend the night, talking with the tides, until the first morning star deposes it.

Two cities once rose beneath it, Messina and Reggio Calabria, but little remains today of their faded glory. On calm evenings, specters of the ancient inhabitants chase one another from shore to shore, descend from the Hills of Neptune and escape to the flat land or dive into the sea that has betrayed them. The water with its shadows, myths, and monsters remains indifferent to their raging, but the voices will torment my sleep until the sirocco returns to silence them; then, perhaps, I'll find some peace. With every new moon I bury my ghosts, but they return, alive and troubling, depending on the winds, on the ephemeris, and on small variations that I alone notice.

I've spent all the nights of my life on this shore, and I know every trick of my false horizon: the eyes of those born beside the sea get lost in the infinite, but my sea is different; it pushes you back like a mirror. The wall of another coast blocked my gaze at birth: maybe that's why I've never left, even when the water abused and deceived me, violated my youth and destroyed who I was.

As a girl, I imagined a boy who lived in the city opposite, looking out a window like mine, a solitary boy shut up in a cage like me. His story, mine, and the story of this place are bound together under the water and under the earth, cards from the tarot deck that the wind has jumbled in the dark. Those stories can only be told together.

Out there before us, in the darkest corner of Calabria, where nothing exists any longer, was what eleven years ago he called home.

# THE HANGED MAN

*The position of the man—upside down, head below, hanging by one foot in a porch, with his free leg folded back at the knee and his arms bound behind his back—at first naturally evokes ideas of gravitation and of the torture that conflict with it can inflict on man.*

There's something stronger than pain, and it's habit.

They say you don't get used to pain, but it's not true: everyone gets used to pain, to inflicting it, to enduring it in an invisible and anesthetizing daily dilution. In the Fera family, who lived in Piazza San Filippo in Reggio Calabria, pain and horror were the air of every day, but Nicola, at eleven, didn't know it: simply, he'd never breathed a different one.

On Sunday, December 27, 1908, after dinner, his mother brought the Torrone di Bagnara to the table. The mixture of honey, egg white, cocoa, and toasted almonds smelled of Christmas celebrations. Outside the windows the carriages were silent, and darkness had descended to end an unexpectedly warm winter day. Maria Fera leaned over her son and, putting her hands on the plate, broke off an outsize piece of torrone.

"I know, it's never enough for you," she screeched, brushing the disheveled blond hair off her forehead; then, grinding her teeth, she began watching him obsessively. "You like torrone so much, I'll have to take it away from you," she insisted. The child was afraid that the candy would stick to his molars and his palate, but, submissive to the voice of his mother the sentinel, he broke it into pieces and chewed as slowly as he could. There was a rule he knew well: whatever he wanted, his mother would claim that he wanted the opposite; he could only go along with her and hope, every time, that it would end soon. The more Nicola obeyed, the more insatiable Maria appeared; the more compliant he was, the more capricious she became. It was always like that, for everything, from school to meals: it was mother's love, the only love the child had experienced, a feeling that took possession of all time and space. Ever since Maria had been blessed with a son, she had devoted her life to him, and never stopped repeating: Don't be ungrateful or Jesus will be disappointed.

Her husband, Vincenzo, on the other hand, concerned with making money in trade, occupied the space and time outside the house, in the city and the entire world. At Christmastime, he and Nicola had spent some hours walking, admiring the windows on Corso Garibaldi and then going on to the Marina, to the market, to buy sugar and raisins. They also went to the Carmelite convent, and to the church of Santa Maria delle Grazie, to see the crèche and ask God's forgiveness and indulgence, without ever specifying for what, in fact being careful not to look each other in the face when they uttered the word "sin." In the view of the people of Reggio, you couldn't ask for a better family: the father with his well-groomed mustache, perfectly pressed overcoat, and the inevitable walking stick capped by the head of an ivory Great

Dane, and behind him his son, a skinny boy in short pants, gaze fixed on the ground, straight brown hair falling over pale skin, against which dark eyes and long, girlish lashes stood out. A perfect harmony, an excellent upbringing: lucky, that Fera, he'd been smart to take a Venetian wife, even if some, finding her scrawny and slightly deformed, had called her a witch. No, she was certainly a good mother, solicitous and attentive, anyway—not even the children of the nobility grew up as polite as Nicolino. All of Reggio thought so, but, if the gossips could have heard the silence between Vincenzo and Nicola, they would have found not two relatives but two strangers, faithful to the duty to make an appearance on holidays. Maria held the monopoly on relations and feelings in the family, hers the power, hers the allotment of affections. As for Vincenzo, the curtains, the porcelain, and the obligation to pay the servants belonged to him: in the family he was the owner of everything and the commander of nothing.

In recent years Vincenzo's bergamot had become the most famous in all of Italy. Nicola, a subscriber to the children's Sunday weekly *Giornalino della Domenica*, had become used to seeing his own surname appear in the advertisement at the end of every episode of the adventures of the *Cadetti di Guascogna—Cadets of Gascony*—where a dark, long-haired lady with a sensuous mouth clutched a vial of Fera perfume. (The anonymous woman was named Giulia, and she had been his nurse, although she was so heavily made up on those pages she seemed another person.) His father always said that men bought two bottles of perfume, one for their wife and one for their mistress, and if they had daughters the purchases multiplied: from Brescia to Palermo, from the Po to the Simeto, in the streets, at the receptions, at the theater, all the women of Italy smelled of Reggio Calabria. Vincenzo Fera could boast of that success, for from a field of *femminello* lemons he had created the perfect essence. He had had the idea as a young man and had made money quickly, then, after snubbing the daughters of the local elite and their dowries, he had gone to the Veneto to take a wife from one of his wealthiest clients, to be sure of establishing the sales in that area. In order not to make a mistake, not to marry a woman who would bring troubles or betrayal, he had taken the ugliest creature of that lineage: at nineteen Maria already had the same sickly, snarling aspect she had in December of 1908. The blonde with the demonic expression, daughter of landowners, had left Verona and her country house in the neighborhood of San Bonifacio to go as a bride to Reggio Calabria, not much interested in love but imbued with the desire to assert herself over men ever since she'd beaten her older brothers with sticks stolen from the woodpile. Marrying a merchant who was ugly, hunchbacked, and twenty years older meant immediately becoming sovereign of the house and the entire Strait, and no one in the vicinity was surprised to see her leave, pursuing that promise. Meanwhile Vincenzo, until then busy by day expanding his business and by night enjoying himself in the brothels, had found the right woman: a scrawny harridan with the eyes of an owl. No one would have touched her.

The family originated in a contract, and so it functioned, with an exclusive mixture of formal agreements, perversions, and complicity. The story of the meeting between Mamma and Papa had been repeated to Nicola like a fable. Over time it had become a legend romantically scented with bergamot, a love that had to strive to be blessed by a birth, because there were no children at first. "That's why your mother loves you so much. See how fortunate you are? Others don't have anyone who protects them the way I protect you," Maria whispered to him at night. When she spoke in an artificially high voice, she twisted her mouth, so that every attempt to clothe herself in sweetness was grotesque. Gracelessness was an ineradicable part of her, and her accent gave her voice the nature of a storm, with thunderclaps and cataclysms and valleys and stillnesses within which her son couldn't move but only let himself be buffeted by the winds.

The evening of December 27th, Nicola went on chewing torrone as if he were swallowing poison with every bite, while Vincenzo, a stranger to everything that concerned his wife and son, lighted a cigarette and slumped back in his chair, stretching his legs, satisfied. That day, too, he had been a good father. The curtain would come down on Sunday, and not only that, the Christmas week would be over: the following day the child would go back to school, at least until the new year, and for him work would begin again, with the inspections for the first consignments of 1909, which for bergamot were forecast to increase. Again.

Maria's eyes didn't leave her son even for a moment. With one finger Nicola picked up the last few almonds from his plate, and, finally, when nothing remained of the torrone, he looked up for permission from his mother, and at a nod went to his father to kiss his hand. The tobacco that saturated Vincenzo's knuckles mingled with the taste of honey. Nicola lowered his head, bowed to both parents, left the room, entered the garden, went along the path among the plants, and arrived at his trapdoor.

The squeaking of the door as it opened broke the silence of the night.

As Nicola set off down the stairs it seemed to him that Maria was still staring at him; her gaze was a goad in his back, chasing the child down, farther and farther down, step by step, between damp walls, toward every night's destiny: the bier set up for him in the cellar.

Descending the stairs was a nightly ceremony, a journey to the center of the Earth, down to the last step, where Nicola stopped, waiting for his eyes to adjust to the darkness. As soon as he could discern the contours of the bier, he made his way into his personal cave and sat on the floor to take off his shoes and his clothes. Barefoot, he went to the basin to wash his feet and hands. He was comfortable in the darkness, in the repetition, in the fantasy of sleeping among the mice, in the ritualization of fear. An animal slid along the wall, maybe a reptile, maybe an insect. Better not to think about it and climb to safety on the high bed his parents had thought up for him. Nicola washed in the darkness, making more noise than necessary and splashing to keep the monsters away with the lapping sound. The cold water gave him goosebumps, and he shivered uncontrollably. He put the basin back and settled himself on the bier, where he covered himself up to his chin. His father's invisible face, smoke puffing from his half-closed mouth, and his mother's, eyes bulging, nailed him where he was, laid to rest with no possibility of resurrection.

Alone, without a light, he stared at the ceiling and began to wait.

Maria's will was the power that ruled his days. It was the devil who suggested escape, and he had to restrain him, repent, be ashamed of the desire for flight and mortify the instinct. Jesus, make me more obedient in the new year, he asked, make me love my mother as she deserves. Yet he couldn't help thinking how sweet it would be, in that prisonlike darkness, to have a window, to let in the innocent air of evening rather than the damp oxygen of an underground hiding place. There was a comforting pile of copies of the *Giornalino della Domenica* at the foot of the funeral monument that was his bed; besides the serial stories, he enjoyed the letters from other children, which made him like all the children in Italy, and he would have liked to read at night, too, to feel them close down there, but no, it was impossible, the night was the night, with its inviolable rules. So Nicola sighed, thinking that the two opposing forces fighting within him, devotion and bewilderment, might kill him. Near the magazines were the remains of a feast of Talmone chocolate from the night before, to please his mamma: the poor didn't have any, Maria pointed out, while his every desire could be fulfilled. How lucky, no? Nicola ran his tongue over the residue of honey between his teeth. Chocolate and torrone were the dream of children all over the world and he would never be without them.

Then the voice of Maria arrived.

"Here he is, my sweetheart, how good he is, and how he loves his mamma."

The words advanced along with the sound of her footsteps; Nicola huddled under the covers.

"My little one who wants to stay with his mamma forever, because he knows that otherwise she would die of grief."

The darkness was filled with the scent of bergamot: Maria's dress was impregnated with it, like the curtains, the tablecloths, and every fabric in the house.

"Tonight, too, Mamma's taking care of you, so you won't be stolen by devils or bad women: you know how many there are around; bad, childless women who want the children of others, the handsomest. I have to stay alert, because no one is handsomer than you."

Now Maria was next to the bed, leaning over him, her mouth stretched toward his ear.

"But you mustn't worry, the Madonna and I are protecting you—we won't let anyone steal you. The Madonna will help me, and you'll stay here with your parents."

Maria took the holy ropes out of her pockets. The first memory of his life stood out clearly in his mind, as it did every night, among countless lacking outlines: his mother grabbing pieces of rope from the hands of the men pulling the Vara, the cart dedicated to the Assumption of the Virgin, in Messina, while he and his father waited in the crowd until the procession ended. The fame of the mid-August procession, in which a cart carries a Madonna who ascends to heaven among dozens of little angels, had convinced Maria Fera that she had to cross the Strait with her family, join the Messinese procession, and, like the other faithful, seize the ropes that pulled the cart from one part of the city to the other. It was said that they had miraculous properties, that they healed the sick, granted wishes.

Nicola stretched his arms above his head, moving his body as far down as possible toward the foot of the bed. Maria took a rope, wound it three times around her son's slender wrists, and gave a tug. A grimace escaped Nicola. Maria caught it in the darkness and quivered with satisfaction.

"No, no, sweetheart, it doesn't really hurt, it keeps away evil." Nicola squeezed his eyelids again and waited for the second rope. Maria leaned over, just above his belly button, pulled down the covers, and immediately the child's body was soaked by the damp air. His mother passed the rope over his stomach and tied it to a leg of the bier. Finally, with the third, she bound his ankles.

"You emptied your bladder, right? You won't wet your bed anymore?"

Nicola nodded his head and Maria pulled up the covers.

He had to sleep in the cellar and not upstairs in the light-filled room with the toys; at least, if the devil came looking for him, he wouldn't find him. He had to be bound because if the devil did find him he wouldn't be able to carry him off. He had to spend the night in a coffin because the devil would be deceived, taking him for dead, and would go and look for other children in other houses. This Maria had explained to him countless times, and Nicola could only respect such scrupulous protection. You know how much I wanted you, she repeated, and again: you didn't want to come, the devil didn't want you to be born, but finally, because I prayed and prayed to the Madonna, you arrived and I deserved my prize.

"Tomorrow morning Mamma will come and wake you early so we can go to school. You're not afraid, right?"

Nicola was about to speak when the voice of Maria became a whisper.

"I prayed to the Madonna for you, and she'll stay with you all night. The devil won't come, and if he does he won't be able to do anything to you."

She said something more as she was leaving, but Nicola heard only "my love, my love," and at last he closed his eyes and made an effort to give himself up to sleep.

# THE MOON

*[T]he eighteenth Arcanum of the Tarot invites us to a spiritual exercise—to a meditation on that which arrests evolutionary movement and tends to give it a direction in an inverse sense. And just as the dominant and principal theme of the seventeenth Arcanum is the agent of growth, so is it a matter in the eighteenth Arcanum of the special agent of diminution—the principle of the eclipse.*

All the doors of childhood had been loose on their hinges, so whenever one started banging I felt it as familiar; its closing and not closing was simply life. On the last night of my being twenty, the door of a railway carriage swayed and grated, its swaying and grating superimposed on the clanking of the wheels and the irritated exchanges of the two other travelers: my contemporaries, yet already husband and wife, quarreling next to me about the education of their daughter and the hand-painting of the china. I didn't care a thing about conjugal affairs; I endured my captivity on the train that would bring us to Messina Centrale, counting backward the time that separated me from the city, the theater, and my grandmother. She—I was sure—would help me find a way out of the trouble I'd brought on myself, choosing to rebel against my father that very afternoon and leave with my heart stirred up and a desire never to return. Meanwhile I shuddered: I couldn't bear my intimacy with the couple, an intimacy made more acute by seats that were too close together. Keys had never functioned for me, I had never enjoyed the privacy of a place that was exclusively mine. The keys of the house in Scaletta Zanclea were all disobedient: in summer they refused to adhere to locks that expanded in the heat; in winter they rusted in the dampness and the salt air; then, when the northeast wind shook doors and shutters, the muggy heat deformed the bolts, the chains sweated, and opposing currents swelled them excessively, the doors of the rooms slammed and, in the in-between seasons, broke.

On the train, the din of the broken door muffled half the sentences, and the dialogue between my seat neighbors assumed the air of a just interrupted or just resumed exchange. I reconstructed the missing words by writing in the white space between answer and question: she, sharp chin and untidy hair, noticed a milk stain on her bust only after the train had departed, and blamed the child's throwing up; he kept on about his wife's faults, accusing her of having chosen the wrong dishes, and of not being the mother their daughter deserved. I hoped that the two would give themselves time to change the fate of that acrimony, that they wouldn't let it fester: like me they were fleeing the towns of the coast for the worldly festivities of the city, and perhaps they would rise above their small miseries and return with their hearts refreshed. Yes, the new year would be a new beginning. Certainly hoping so for them was easier than hoping so for myself.

We were escaping the provinces in the same way, despite the fact that we weren't the same: they had a favorable wind of proper choices, they had been joined before God, had reproduced, hadn't disregarded social and familial expectations, and even their stubborn unhappiness was perfect; that marriage functioned and didn't function, in the manner of all marriages. An unsteady door separated us and, swaying, marked the division of the two worlds: they could talk and expose themselves, I was shy and couldn't even read, and yet we were making the same journey and shared its origin, the winter of marginal creatures. In order to survive, they had chosen marriage and I books, so it would always be like that: I was forced to listen to them and they were not compelled even to see me, even at the moment when we were fleeing together to the city to nourish ourselves on its mirages. I hoped that in Messina, amid the lights of the port, they would regain their lost compassion, the mercy necessary to tolerate each other for the rest of their lives, but ultimately it didn't concern me; I concentrated on my own trouble. I turned my eyes away from the door and my ears from the sounds to give my senses to the sea outside the window: the waves muffled voices and jangling, and the memory of what I had just done, of the strength I had managed to find, emerged clearly.

My father had come with me to the station and, walking beside him, I had told him that I wouldn't marry the man he had chosen for me. He didn't answer. My steps became violent, my wait crushing: I wished to be seen, to hear myself shout that I was depraved and corrupted. If he had ordered me to throw away the novel I had in my bag, at least he would have given a shape to who I was: a girl who had learned courage from books and, seeing herself in the women recounted by women, had chosen to resemble certain rebel heroines who avoided the fate written for them. Instinctively I clutched the handles of my bag to indicate to my father the hiding place of my desire. But his expression didn't change, it was as if no one had spoken. I was no one, not a body or a voice, only baggage to be taken to the station, deposited on a train, sent to Messina, and sent back the next day. That in the depths of that bag there was a book, and in the depths of my body the desire for another life, mattered only to me.

On the platform, before letting me go, my father had made sure that no one entered the car who might have been able to annoy or distract me. His eyes had constructed around my body a cage to keep away frivolous men or women; finally he had approved the harmless young couple who were climbing up the step. It had seemed to me then that my father, simply by his presence, had the power to control what happened to me, and the rage of the invisible mounted in me. That was the only family I felt I belonged to, the family of people who can't choose for themselves because they don't have a platform or even a prayer stool, but are placed forcibly in a gilded chair by a god they haven't chosen. My father was my God and I didn't adore him. I had taken out *Maria Landini* and had put it in his hands: read it, I'd said, read it and you'll see me. He stepped aside, and Letteria Montoro's book ended up on the sidewalk; we were left facing each other with the novel between us. The one who bent down to pick it up would be declared the loser, and my father didn't want to lose; he didn't want to play or even sanction the competition.

I leaned over to get the book and my fingers touched the station dust. He reproached me for saying foolish things, and his words were inscribed on my curved back, finally crushing it.

My father did not hesitate to rebuff me. He didn't know that escapes to the city and into books had allowed me to survive my childhood, my mother's death, and the cold winters. In Messina, at my grandmother's house and in her company, I became a little older each time, while everywhere, even in the solitude of Scaletta, novels were mother and knife, caress and weapon, unexpected pathways, the only keys that had ever opened doors. Maria Landini, the protagonist of the book he had refused even to touch, didn't marry the cruel baron Summacola for whom she was destined, and, to avoid that marriage, ran away from her family. If he had read about her he would have seen my desertion; instead, to his eyes I remained a blur. My father arranged women in the display case of functions: wife, mother, daughter, old maid; position and lineage counted, being humble and careful to move aside at the proper moment. As for love, either it was productive or it wasn't. He had promised me to an ugly, stupid man, who would have kept me sealed in a house not mine where I would have grown gracefully like mold on a wall, concerning myself with sofas, china cupboards, and children. The protagonists of the novels I loved rejected that fate with acts of heroism, paying the consequences, while I was unable even to make my voice heard. Now that I had had the courage to do it, my voice wasn't listened to.

"Tell my mother that I'll come and visit next week, and that tonight, after the theater, I would prefer that she bring you home right away. You have enough entertainments; you should begin to take a little responsibility."

They were my father's last words. It was pointless to add more: I confined myself to saying goodbye obediently and thanking him for allowing me this evening's pleasure, then I took my place on the train with the idea of never returning to his house and his control.

The train arrived on time at Messina Centrale.

The couple passed by in front of me without having acknowledged me for the whole journey, too absorbed in their shared unhappiness to make room for my existence; if those were the looks from which, according to my father, I should have felt protected, it wasn't surprising that I had learned quickly to get along by myself. I crossed the station hall and was outside.

High in the sky, a sliver of crescent moon lit up the Hills of Neptune and extended over the remains of the Royal Palace, easing my fatigue. The silver rays loosened the knot that weighed in my heart, urging me to rebirth as I advanced amid carriages and lamp-lighters, the clatter of horses' hooves and the magic of the lights coming on. With every step I imagined the girl I wanted to become, I sought the courage to plant my eyes in those of others, not only my father's but also my grandmother's; to her I would unburden myself, asking her advice. I dreamed of forcibly rejecting the man whose surname I didn't even want to utter; in any case it would never be mine. I walked, head high, in the Messina evening, the voice inside me growing always louder, firmer, my breast more prominent: I was transformed into rock, into one of the cliffs of the crescent-shaped part of the city, I would hold back the winds and stop the waters, conquering the opposing currents.

My father, born in one of the most beautiful houses of the Palazzata—the huge, majestic baroque structure on the harbor that welcomed sailors from the Strait—had chosen to move away from urbanity and establish himself in Scaletta Zanclea, a town on the coast, at the proper distance. As for me, he tolerated my going to the city only because it meant that I would spend time with my grandmother, who would also be a mother to me, as I no longer had a mother. Principally, he had to safeguard me at all costs. After the death of his wife, after her illness had defeated him, because he had been unable to keep her alive, his guardianship of me had become the measure of his existence. But for me going to Messina meant something else: I tore a hole in a dull barricade of days that were all the same. In the town I had only the company of books and the sea, while in the city there was a celebration at every moment: theater, ocean liners, libraries, stores, professors, students, the university I imagined attending. Some mornings I went there secretly, slipping into the last rows of the literature classes in the room where, a few years earlier, the poet Giovanni Pascoli had taught: my grandmother had known him and had his books in her house. I opened them, read the dedications, and dreamed of one day signing the title page of a novel. Unfortunately the university wasn't a place for girls, and if my father had known that I went there, not to mention with the complicity of his mother, no young couple would have been enough to persuade him to let me get on a train for Messina. My grandmother, however, had a different idea about the need for my education, and knew what was best not to mention to her son.

Beside the port a sailor in uniform looked at me as if he wanted to eat me.

"*Heavenly Aida, divine form, Mystical garland of light and flowers,*" he began singing, then broke off and laughed hard without touching me. He wanted to scare me, as men did with us women, so that we wouldn't forget who was in charge, inside and outside the house. Even if we dared to go out alone, the streets were not to be ours even for a moment. "*You are the queen of my thoughts, You are the splendor of my life*": I continued the interrupted lines in my head. I can't sing in tune and was afraid of signaling availability, so my mouth didn't move, but inside I sang, even though I never hit the right note and my rhythm was off, because I liked music and envied those who mastered it. To troublesome courtships, on the other hand, I was accustomed, and I kept going, trying to disappear into the crowd while Radamès's song remained suspended, hovering between my silence and the voices of evening. Then it seemed to me that every passerby, every horse, every window was starting to sing the opera that was playing, a story of love, war, and betrayal, and I felt that that story of sacrifices might concern us all, in every epoch and every place, and that the woman determined not to retreat from her feelings could be, in a different way, another of my heroines. My grandmother had a family box at the Vittorio Emanuele theater, and that evening we would occupy it together; besides, we always went together, as my parents had never been interested in the theater, or in music or art, whereas I liked opera librettos, novels in miniature that populated my days. After I'd seen a performance, the actors would break up the isolation of my room in the town; they came to sing for me above the bed and the chest of drawers, among the chairs and the mirrors, rearranging the trinkets and the hairbrush, hiding in the closets, on the breakfast tray. When I returned from Messina after seeing an opera I was no longer alone, the men and women in costume continued to move around me on imaginary stages, for weeks and months and sometimes forever. And yet there had to be a way to live without being crushed into the corner where my father wanted to banish me, there had to be a way to make those characters true and concrete, transform them into people.

On the way to my grandmother's house the passersby grazed me with their overcoats and smiled, I heard their voices, the excitement, the fragments of conversation, and I saw that I would be happy just to stay here, with Italy across the Strait, observing the traffic of the ferry boats that docked and departed; I would be free to go to the theater to see *Aida*, free to sing and be out of tune, to walk along the Palazzata and not be afraid of the arrogance of men.

My father's mother had my name, Barbara, because of a legendary family story that I would have liked to make into a novel. That story, told countless times, began with a cruise ship that disembarked at Messina and an English noblewoman who, distracted by the beauties of the city and in particular by the bell tower of the Duomo, had by a miracle avoided being struck by a carriage. But her hem got caught under one of the wheels and dragged her toward the street. She nearly fell; then the dress tore and she remained standing. A rescuer suggested to the frightened visitor the address of the best seamstress of the two seas, who was known simply as 'a maestra, the master. When the noblewoman knocked at the door, she was greeted by a skinny young woman wearing a light-brown dress, a little lighter than her hair, which was gathered in a braid. It was a very plain dress, without frills or anything gaudy about it, and gave her a natural look. Everything about her shone with an unostentatious care. 'A maestra hadn't wanted to neglect the talent she'd had since she was a girl: her fingers slid magically over silk and muslin, she seemed to be the interpreter of a superior will that enabled her to subjugate every fabric. In her hands, the Englishwoman's dress was mended, as if the accident had never happened. Meanwhile, the two had begun speaking in a vocabulary of their own—one knew no foreign language, the other little Italian, and yet they entrusted to whispers and gestures a desire to know each other arising from the solitude of those who are used to keeping to themselves a lively intelligence, containing it in their own inner world. They mirrored each other in that particular form of love that is friendship and, when the noblewoman looked at the other's belly, the seamstress confirmed that, yes, it was a five months' belly, and since it was round it would be a female. She wouldn't accept money for the mending; sewing for her was a passion and not a trade, and she didn't need money. Helping women was her personal task, as well as her way of not letting her life be stolen by a marriage that otherwise could have nullified her. The foreigner had asked if she could repay her in hospitality, and invited her to England, but crossing the Strait was not in the *maestra's* plans, journeys were not for her, she preferred to stay on her island, in her house, in the rooms where she welcomed her sisters. Rather, I'll give the child your name, she said, so you'll be here in Messina with me forever. And she kept the promise: four months later, my great-grandmother *maestra* gave birth to a healthy newborn who was given an odd English name. Thus began the lineage of Barbaras: my name was rooted in the Strait like an exotic plant.

Then, compared with the delicacy of that story, society must have closed up again, or maybe it was the Ruellos who turned in on themselves after the early death of my grandfather, because of my father's anxiety to control everything, to occupy the vacant role of head of the family. In Scaletta I was called Rina, short for Barbarina: my mother, for the very few years she was with me, preferred it to differentiate me from her mother-in-law, my father to remind me that I was smaller than my name, not a complete Barbara. For him I would become whole after marriage: marrying, I would gain a new surname, and only then take possession of my name as well. As for my grandmother, she was the only one who called me Barbara, undaunted even in front of her son, who had once dared to correct her: we call her Rina. And she, immediately: I will call my granddaughter what I like, I'll call her by my name. However, before she was Barbara Ruello, my grandmother had been Signorina Todaro, and, no matter how important she considered my wholeness in freedom, she didn't forget that the double surname was the fate of every woman.

I, on the other hand, would have liked Ruello to be enough forever.

# THE DEVIL

*The ideas that are evoked by the totality of the Card and its context are rather those of slavery, in which two personages are found who are attached to the pedestal of a monstrous demon. The Card does not suggest the metaphysics of evil, but rather an eminently practical lesson as to how it happens that beings can forfeit their freedom and become slaves of a monstrous entity which makes them degenerate by rendering them similar to it.*

A wave moves under the black covers, a lump rises, forms a hill, the small pyramid aims at the ceiling, tosses and turns, and finally reveals itself: it's a beast, and it's groaning. That pyramid is the snout of an animal.

Nicola raises himself on his elbows, pushes the covers away, and finds a bloodstained white cat staring at him, meowing, begging him for words, and, while he longs to, he can't teach it any alphabet. He keeps digging with his hands, digs with the little strength he has in sleep, until he disinters a second cat, striped, with scratches all around the tiny eyes; the mouth is cut, surrounded by small wounds, cuts. But it's alive. It meows and meows. A miracle that it wasn't suffocated to death under the other one, which blocked it, crushing its head, lacerating it with bites and claw marks.

Now both animals are free, the dominant white and the other, the wounded tiger. The blanket that enveloped them is far away, the bleeding cat scratches on the tiles, the violent cat's cries are transformed into a tingling that travels along the palm of Nicola's hand, into a whistle in his ears so loud the child has to wake up.

It happened every night. Once he was alone, rather than sinking into an isolated unconsciousness, Nicola began to suffer from the ropes around his wrists. He let his fingertips challenge the limits of flesh. While the darkness ate the air in his lungs, an invisible force shook his body, and a presentiment of death flooded the cellar. He fell asleep like that, between visions and terrors, until, punctually, the nightmares arrived.

He woke that night, too, alarmed by a child wailing. He tried to pull himself up to save the child, but the ropes reminded him that he couldn't, and the lament turned out to be a meow: somewhere on the earth's surface a cat was howling like a wolf at the moon. Nicola struggled to separate the pounding of his heart from the sounds and contours of reality. Was there really an animal outside the cellar? Where were the cats he had dug up in his dream? Were there creatures whose footsteps he was hearing? The damp air was saturated with little noises.

In some of the fables Maria read to Nicola, you had only to clap your hands to move from one country to another, from a house to a castle, from a prison to freedom. A clap of the hands was enough for an act of magic. At night, however, with his wrists bound, not even that simple movement was possible; only his eyelashes were free. He opened his eyelids and closed them, reopened them and closed them again, and continued until he was awake and conscious. Then he imagined expanses of air, water, land; he saw himself planting his palms and his neck on a meadow, pushing down on his toes, raising his heels to the sky, and letting go in a crooked somersault while the sun obstinately pierced his bones. He felt his legs getting hot, but it wasn't the sun, it was the blankets, and he felt like crying. Hold it, hold it in, he repeated to himself, feeling his mother's murky gaze on him, but the harder he held it in, the harder the force of muscular contraction pulled in the opposite direction, dismembering him, so that he felt one with the air. Centimeter by centimeter Nicola yielded under a weight that was crushing him to the bottom, until he realized that without the ropes he would bore into the bier and end up a dead weight on the floor or even farther down. If he had been untied, then, yes, he would have been in danger, falling disjointedly, his body twisted and awry.

The nightmares, his personal nighttime dirt, Nicola recalled one by one. A knife stuck in the railing of the balcony, the night he'd fallen asleep after reading a pirate story. A small, bug-eyed girl with a man's hoarse loud voice returned often to visit him. A furry animal whose cut-off tail kept moving on its own, near the stump. The shed on a terrace that concealed a newborn: Nicola opened the door, dusted the furniture, and the sun cut the room in two, leaving space for a wail, while at his feet lay a bundle of blankets. Finally, two opposing, complementary cats that, fighting, sketched out on the ground games of power and subjugation.

Now Nicola could open his eyes. No blinking of eyelashes, no journeys in his head, the sweet darkness became the unpleasant voice of Maria. Her closed vowels echoed with rancor, her drawn-out words, as long and smooth as corridors, forming sentences whose meaning Nicola couldn't grasp but only the tentacular sound of a clanging, roaring monster. A creature half jellyfish and half snarl arrived above the bier and, stopping a few centimeters from his face, opened a gigantic mouth full of sharp teeth. His mother's voice devoured him. Then Nicola felt nothing, and afterward a heap of bristly hairs ran over his neck, the tips of Maria's dry blond hair. The nightmare was over, he was in his mother's arms. Nicola pulled on the ropes in an attempt to free himself, this time to surround that small thorny body, but again he was defeated. Salvation, like damnation, was only an illusion. He tasted the hot chocolate of Caffè Spinelli on winter afternoons when, after Mass, Maria took Nicola to drink his reward. They entered together, his mother took off his coat, hello Signora, how the *picciriddu* has grown, hello, what weather this is. Chat of women above the smoke of important people sitting fixed at their tables, making a show of reading the evening papers. The stagnant smell of cigars and cakes pierced by Fera perfume, so Maria always presented herself, reminding everyone of who she was and her power; Nicola felt disgust at that scent of bergamot and stuck his nose in the cup of hot chocolate, licked it with the tip of his tongue, and for a moment was far away and happy.

Blink of the eyelids, another round, another oasis. Summer at the beach, the euphoria of the salt air, and here he is climbing up the monument to the rebels. But childish games and shouts weren't supposed to disturb that serious tribute; Maria had sighed with relief when the mayor put up a bar to keep children away from the statue.

Another blink, another round. The night Maria and Vincenzo argued about the phylloxera that was devastating the vineyards. They were so impassioned they skipped dinner. Nicola was at the table, and for once he had been able to eat without someone looking at his plate: the taste of freedom was the taste of prosciutto and oil, without the bread that every night Maria put in front of him saying that it had been blessed by God. He didn't like divine bread, even though he was ashamed to confess it even to himself.

Final blink, final happy moment: Vincenzo had been invited as a guest of honor to the inauguration of the new electric lighting system and had brought him along. The switching on of the electrical system seemed like a conjuror's trick, and, while his father was busy greeting his acquaintances, Nicola admired the way the colors tinted the air over the Strait.

Maria and Vincenzo, Vincenzo and Maria: the oppressors were two, but they presented themselves as one, like the figure that appeared on the table the night his mother had taken him to the fortune teller.

Let's go see a lady who will help us, she had said on the afternoon of Christmas the year before, because I can't do it alone, and your father doesn't give me enough help. A wind was blowing in the dry air, and as they went farther from the city center there were fewer people and the sirocco grew stronger. They were bundled up, in clothes too heavy for that warm wind, and when they reached a low house, with dark windows, they took off scarves and hats. Maria put them in her purse, which became distended and heavy. She knocked three times at the door. My cousin is in the other room, she's expecting you, said a woman with a long bumpy nose, and mother and son found themselves in a living room with flowered chairs set around a gilded iron table. Madame, so Maria addressed her, had come from Marseilles a few days earlier; she was a robust woman, with a large chest and lively almond-shaped eyes, dressed all in white lace. She knew the Arcana, she'd known how to read them since she was a child. She was the granddaughter of fortune tellers, but, rather than the nighttime appearance of a magician, she had a fresh laugh and an intense and frank expression. She appeared amused by the commotion in the house of her relatives, and still a little dazed by the journey. She uttered her words with a French accent, but her Italian was excellent, her voice a mixture of honey and cinnamon.

"A girl your age was just here," she said to Nicola. "Do you like girls?"

"He's very shy," Maria quickly answered for him.

"So, what's the problem with this child?" Madame asked.

"His father and I love him above all else, but Nicola doesn't understand that; and he doesn't realize that the world is full of dangers, he thinks he can go around by himself."

Madame had observed mother and son and shuffled the pack of cards, then she cut it in two and displayed the card: the Devil. Maria jumped up triumphant: I told you, see, see if you run away what will happen to you?

The fortune teller's eyes then fell on Nicola, Nicola's on the card: he saw a creature with horns and wings, half devil and half angel, with a woman's breast and between his legs the sex of men, sitting on a throne with chains around his ankles, which reached the feet of two small helpers, a male devil and a female, both in miniature. The little devils looked at the big one as if they expected to receive orders from him. Nicola looked up at Madame. She returned a gaze full of compassion and started to say something.

"How much do I owe you?" Maria intervened, with uncontainable delight.

"The consultation doesn't require money," Madame answered, rendered silent.

Maria opened her purse and left a bottle of Fera perfume on the table. Then she said goodbye and, trotting along the street with Nicola following, reminded him at every step: "Did you see that the Devil wants to get you? Now you've seen it, too." But Nicola couldn't stop thinking of the Devil's two small helpers: male and female, Vincenzo and Maria.

Who knows if Madame was in Reggio Calabria that Christmas, too. Who knows if now, in the night of cat-wolves howling at the moon, she was in the low house, if she had received people, if she had cut the cards for them. Who knows what was drawn on the other cards, the ones they hadn't seen, and what it would have been like to cut them, throw them all on the table and be able to choose one's own.

Nicola returned to perceiving his body. His buttocks were stuck to his underpants, the underpants stuck to the sheets, while the ceiling no longer existed, and he could see the sky and the sweetness of the moon.

He had wet the bed and the night wasn't over yet.

# THE EMPEROR

*Now, the Emperor of the fourth Arcanum of the Tarot
does not have a sword or any other weapon. He rules
by means of the* sceptre, *and by the sceptre alone.
This is why the first idea that the Card naturally
evokes is that of the* authority *underlying* law.

Slave and princess, beloved and prisoner, daughter and lover: Aida,
suspended between opposites, appeared to me in the theater incomplete and fickle, while I was disoriented by Amneris, the deceived,
who, by means of signs visible only to intuition, discovers the affair
between her slave and her beloved. I was on her side, the embittered, abandoned, and betrayed Amneris, the heroine thrust into
the tragedy of another woman, who steals her fiancé along with
the place of honor in her story. I was vexed by the female rivalry
stirred up by the text, I was annoyed that two women had to fight
over a man, a soldier who wasn't even so valuable, who had already
proved unworthy of one and might have disappointed the other as
well: both seemed like marionettes controlled by the power of men,
incited to hatred of each other and dragged into ruin.

During the performance, Grandmother never once turned to

look at me. Everything about her behavior was unusual; even the way she greeted me when I arrived at her house had struck me. She was irritated, she said, because I had refused to take the earlier train and now we might be late. I had never known her angry with me, and apologized in confusion. I placed my bag on the bed in the guest room and changed quickly, instinctively choosing, between the two outfits I had brought, the one with the higher neck, which covered me more fully. The theater was near her house, and during the short walk Grandmother didn't say a word to me, greeting friends and acquaintances but continuing to ignore me.

I tried to concentrate on the performance, on my vexation with Verdi's opera, which couldn't be shared, on my solitary doubts about what concerned my family and my desires. I tried again to find a way to enjoy the opera, but it seemed impossible. Compelled to be on Aida's side, we were obliged to hate Amneris, as if she were an enemy and not also a victim of conventions, a woman who had to become an informer to save herself from the humiliation of betrayal, because the man she should have married loved someone else. Only marriage legitimized a woman's life, it was said, and if it was true for Princess Amneris certainly it must be for me who was no one.

There was a note of grotesque unreality on the painted faces of the actors, fake Ethiopians who crowded the stage with coal-colored faces, artificial imitations of children in the illustrations in the *Giornalino della Domenica* that entertained me on dark winter afternoons. Here Aida seemed one of those caricatures, just a little older, but she was played by an actress with diaphanous skin: the coloring dripped off with the sweat, and her lost, slightly mystical gaze moved gracefully from the stage to the audience, as if wishing to apologize for the embarrassment that was coming out of her, precisely her, with her body and her complexion. If with half my brain I followed the performance, with the other I invented a form for the actors' silences, I deconstructed the story, I inserted myself between the person and the character, I opened the gap between the invented story and the life, I felt worry and intolerance flying over our heads, beyond the orchestra and the boxes of the Vittorio Emanuele, beyond the square and the Palazzata, beyond the Strait, where I, too, would have liked to flee. The tenor more than once sought my gaze, or at least so I wanted to think, interpreting that gesture in the dark through my wish to exist, to be seen.

My grandmother was never distracted from the stage and never touched my arm while we were sitting beside each other; at the intermission she merely rose, assuming that I would follow her, and ordered two glasses of mint liqueur without asking me what I wanted. With an ill grace I swallowed that cold drink, unsuited to the season: her favorite drink, not mine—I liked the amaro Ferro China. My grandmother's new hostility disoriented me, but I bided my time and said to myself that I would ask her about it calmly, not, certainly, in the lobby, where we were surrounded by people who treated her like a queen and looked at me with greedy, searching curiosity. What was Signora Ruello's granddaughter up to, why wasn't she engaged yet, and why did she always come to the city by herself?

When the final act arrived, I wasn't on the side of Aida or Amneris but was hoping that the color, dripping yet again, would free the faces of the singers and the truth would be bared by the staging. While the odor of death advanced from the stage, my grandmother, hair gathered on her neck, and on her lap the embroidered purse, was moved, in harmony with the rest of the audience: a euphoric energy roused the spectators, and the last word and the last note evoked immediate applause. Grandmother was the first to jump to her feet, weeping along with the others at the death of two lovers buried alive.

Long live love, the voices around me sighed, long live love and long live the nation; the curtain fell on the cave of Aida and Radamès, and Amneris prayed on their grave, shedding tears of forgiveness or regret.

Outside the warm, magnificent night awaited us.

The new electrical system in Reggio produced a luminous reflection in the Strait, and the cities joined by that wake were closer than ever: the moon and the stars seemed to have moved from the sky to the sea, and the entire Milky Way was floating on it. I would have liked to swim amid the water lilies of light, strip off my coat and skirt, loosen my corset, throw off the hat, abandon my shoes on the cliffs, and give my body to the sirens. I wanted to sink in the currents like Cola, the boy with the fish tail, then return to the surface and swim to Calabria, abandoning on the island everything that had to do with my appearance: the carapaces that bound and disguised me, the fabrics that constrained me to an unnatural aesthetic, my gestures and voices when speaking to my family—my father and now, too, my grandmother. Swimming, I would get to the other side and be saved.

In fact I had never crossed the Strait. Of the world I knew only my town and my city; not even the opposite coast was permitted. For a long time I'd wanted to go to Reggio to admire the magic of the ancient Aragonese castle, and I'd asked permission to take the ferry to watch the inauguration of the lights that everyone was talking about, but my father had answered as he always did: it's not the moment, we don't have time. For my father it was never the moment, the right time, and he didn't even add a future, a word to let me hope that one day a different calendar would be there for me. He blocked the answer and moved on: my voice and my question didn't exist.

Meanwhile, in the square there was a continuous clasping and kissing of hands, praise of the performers' skill, greetings sent to the family members who had stayed home, what they'd missed, that *Aida* had been a marvel, so many tears we'd shed, and the two buried alive, what a harrowing image, what a cruel end. Someone had put some chairs in the street for those who had to wait for the end of the leave-taking ceremonies among the worldly, a few old people sat down, a pregnant woman, and me. I had my back to the theater's façade and was looking again at the sea, when an unknown voice called me by name. Before me was the handsomest creature I'd ever seen, so handsome he cut off my breath and blew it away.

"Barbara, I apologize if I'm disturbing you," said a young man. He had a pale complexion, greenish eyes, and fine brown hair, and was dressed with sober elegance. "I didn't mean to frighten you, I've seen you at the university. You're brave to come there—why don't you come to Professor Salvemini's classes, too?"

So someone was aware of my forays into academe. It wasn't enough to sit in the back rows like the sister of a student, avoid taking notes so as not to arouse curiosity, leave a little before the end and slip immediately into the street, to go to Grandmother's house. Someone had seen me and understood that I was there not to wait but to listen.

The creature apologized for bothering me and introduced himself. His name was Vittorio Trimarchi, and he was the assistant of the legendary historian Gaetano Salvemini: for a cultured girl the professor's lectures would be interesting, he insisted, and then he could come and get me and bring me home if it was a problem to go out alone. He would reserve a seat apart for me, no one would bother me, a seat for the entire duration of the course. He said other things, but I was stunned and missed whole sentences. I could think only: a seat just for me at the university, an invisible plate with my name stamped on it. And also: that creature who responded to the name of Vittorio Trimarchi knows who I am, has observed me, has seen me, his large emerald eyes reflecting my figure, my soul. I thanked him and said I would think about it, I would have to ask my family for permission, because I lived in Scaletta Zanclea and spent most of my time there, and if I came to Messina it was only for short periods. But I was strengthened in my convictions: by the start of the new year I will find a way of freeing myself and do what I like without accounting to my father or others. For once I was forced to include my grandmother among the jailers, and that thought was a shadow over me. Vittorio continued to reassure me, he said there was nothing dishonorable about an educated woman, in fact it was right that women should study before getting married: having an intelligent wife was good for a man, equality of intentions and culture was the secret of a long partnership. And as his speeches moved through me, something in me was released, I trusted him with an unknown naturalness, I said little because he said it all, I had no need to add or correct, every word was perfect, like his face; I admired his fine hair, curly in the dampness that came from the harbor. Finally he asked if I'd like to come to his house, he lived with his mother, and they had invited a group of friends and relatives for a post-theater gathering. At that point Grandmother approached and answered for me that it was late, that I was tired because of the journey, even if out of politeness I didn't show it; she emphasized that I was well brought up, certainly I wouldn't want to be rude, and it was up to her to be firm and protect me. Vittorio replied that then they would expect us at lunch the next day, when I had rested. We'll see, Grandmother dismissed him; he wrote the address on a piece of paper that he gave me, but she took it out of my hand and immediately turned her back on him.

This time, during the short walk home, I tried to talk to her. It was now clear that the matter of the marriage to the man whose name I didn't even want to utter was already known to her. My father had acted on his own inclinations, and it wasn't a question of recent pressure but a work rooted in time, which had found fertile ground in her. I tried anyway to appeal to what we had in common, the values in whose name she had brought me up, music, theater, literature, and the disdain for village life that separated her from my father and led her to disagree with his choices. You, I entreated her, you taught me to look for my destiny in what I read. Until she's twenty a woman has to grow, she answered, and then she stops. And she added: with another surname beside yours you'll be able to do everything; with your own name, by yourself, you're nothing. We went in.

I hoped that the crystal chandelier in the living room would come crashing down, that every piece of antique furniture would turn to dust, that no trace would remain of who we had been. I hated every mark of the vaunted antiquity of my family, and went to sleep knowing that for me there was no hope, the only possibility escape.

Around me, the city's din was fading. After the theater the last entertainments were ending in the houses where cards were played: the Messinese with exotic tastes loved baccarat, chemin de fer, and French cards, but for the most part they played Tivitti, that is to say *ti vitti*, "I saw you." It was my favorite game, and had been since I was a child, the game where if a forgetful or distracted player doesn't put down a card, and misses his turn, one more vigilant could report him: I saw you, you're making a mistake, you're not paying attention. *Ti vitti* was the tipoff, the disgrace, and saying it we enjoyed ourselves hugely at the festive Christmas tables. *Ti vitti* was what none of us wanted to hear.

And yet today someone saw me and I would like him to see me tomorrow, too, I thought, before falling asleep. Tranquillity didn't last long, though: I dreamed I was on the stage between Aida and Amneris and I tried to sing but couldn't, not the faintest sound came out of my mouth. I woke up frightened and, after tossing and turning for a long time, tormented by too many thoughts, decided that for me the night ended there.

Looking out the third-floor window I gazed at the sea and the quay outside the living room of my childhood and, alongside, the windows of the other apartments in the Palazzata, all shuttered: the office windows that would stay closed until the end of the Christmas holidays, and those of the houses, where families were sleeping and no one was restless, like me.

I couldn't drive out the face of the man whose surname I wouldn't say, while Vittorio appeared distant, blurred, not even he could soothe me. I repeated the beginning of *Maria Landini*: "The power of suffering alone, the bitter nourishment of my entire life, drove the pen almost in spite of myself." The author warned that her pages would not provide a display of learning or style, but I knew that wasn't true: quotations from Leopardi and Alfieri undergirded the chapters, there was knowledge in the prose. Letteria Montoro had studied, and a lot, careful never to shine too brightly, in order not to attract the envy of men. Her very name had its origins in a story of women and words: in 42 AD the Madonna had sent a message to the Messinese to thank them for their faith and bless them, and a Madonna-writer had therefore become the patron saint of the city, the Madonna della Lettera, Madonna of the Letter. It was she who blessed all us women, and Letteria Montoro had merely followed the destiny stamped in her name. A few weeks before, I had learned from the cemetery caretaker where she was buried. I knew that on the stone she was remembered as "a woman of free spirit," and that description fascinated me; I had promised myself to go and visit her with more time. In the crisp dark December air, I vowed that the next day I would kneel at her grave, I would tell her my story and receive in exchange the good luck of her talented hand, and then I would accept Vittorio Trimarchi's invitation to lunch, with or without my grandmother. I would begin to live as I believed and would become strong-willed and open-minded, I would stop complaining and repeating the same litany, I would pay the price to be who I wanted to be. Along with this premise for the future an unexpected sleepiness returned. By now my legs were stiff, and I decided to go to bed.

An instant before I turned my back to the night, the sea moved.

A polyphony pierced my ears, the floor collapsed along with the remains of my house and with it I plunged into a pile of ruins.

The world as I had known it ended, and everything loved or hated disappeared.

# THE WHEEL OF FORTUNE

*The Card of the tenth Arcanum therefore teaches,
through its actual context, an organism of ideas relating
to the problem of the Fall and the Reintegration,
according to Hermetic and Biblical tradition.*

Nicola Fera opened his eyes while Reggio Calabria was collapsing
on top of him.

The sheet under his buttocks was wet with pee, the roof of the
cellar cracked by the projections of his own nightmares.

In the time it took to prick up his ears the apocalypse had begun.
A Scylla and Charybdis together, a monster with six heads, each dis-
playing three rows of sharp teeth, had risen from the center of the
Strait, had flapped its dragon's tail and razed to the ground the Calabrian shore while the roar of an anomalous thunder set it on fire.

The cellar danced like a submarine, the ceiling threatened to
crash down, and the child dragged his voice out of his lungs, wriggled arms and legs in vain, wounded wrists and ankles but failed
to loosen the ropes that bound him to the bier. He wept until his
throat burned, calling on first one Maria, then the other, mother
and Madonna, to beg forgiveness for every sin committed in his

eleven years of life, even the ones committed in thought—especially those, because impure thought, as we know, leads to vice and misfortune. The evil din eroded his eardrums and entered his small body, a suffocating, murderous sound. To expel it, Nicola arched and flattened his back like the guinea pig of an exorcism, but rubbing against the mattress only caused him to keep wetting his pants. At the same time, near the bed, the room was burning, a bonfire with devils and witches dancing around it, a will o' the wisp that didn't warm and didn't dry. What circle of Hell will I end up in, Nicola wondered, because he knew he was dead, dead and destined to atrocious punishments, that fire was Hell.

After thirty seconds the monster was silent. The fire went out, and the roar diminished.

Then time ceased to exist. Night and day disappeared, clock hands and clocks, devils and witches, bonfires and bleeding cats. In the murky stillness of the silence a fragmentary rumble rose from time to time, a series of miniature versions of the great thunder that had passed, brief new jolts with no voice, no cry. Outside everyone must be dead, people and animals. Dead the objects, the houses, every organism, everything visible and invisible. And Nicola—did he belong to life or death? Where is the line that separates them if no one can hear you?

Maria, Vincenzo, Papa, Mamma, Mamma, Papa, Maria, Vincenzo, the child intoned. Weeping and shouting were a single thing until, as he rubbed and pulled, the tie on his left hand became so thin it broke, and for once the holy ropes had done their duty of salvation. With the patience of his freed fingers, Nicola began to work the right wrist, knot after knot, digging and scratching with his short nails, and when he managed to untie that arm he sat up straight, loosened the bonds on his ankles, jumped down from the bed, and ran to the door.

Mother, father he called: he would save them from the monster, he would arrive in time to carry them away from the house, who knows where, maybe they could go to Mamma's Veneto?

But the trapdoor was blocked. No matter how Nicola tried to force it, using fists and shoulders, it didn't move a millimeter, as if the entire city of Reggio and the promontory of Aspromonte were piled on top of it.

Soaked in tears and urine, without a voice, defeated and hoarse, Nicola crept under the bier, drank from the same basin in which a few hours before he had washed, and went on crying without dignity, because dignity is the thing we need least and is the greatest stumbling block when we feel pain. He drank, thinking he should ration the water, to survive as long as possible: without eating one can live but not without drinking, so he had heard from Maria, the mother jailer who controlled even how much water he left in his glass, the mother eye and monster who in memory had become an angel. If only he had listened to her and hadn't wanted to escape, if he had been good, the end of the world would not have arrived. It was he, Nicola, who had summoned the apocalypse: he wanted to run away, and God had grown angry.

"I ask your forgiveness, Mother, I ask forgiveness from Father, God, and Maria, the very holy Madonna, who in her mercy untied my ropes although I deserved to die," the weeping child repeated. Now and again there was a jolt, the roof shook, and above Nicola's head Piazza San Filippo was still silent.

"Forgive me, Mother, Father, God, and Maria," sometimes he sobbed, other times he dreamed. He no longer knew when he was asleep and when he was awake, if the floor was beneath his neck or behind his back. At times he seemed to see again those cats that had been fighting a little earlier, he heard their shrieks and defended himself from their claws, but they were only dreams, because right afterward he was in the kitchen, where his mother's hand grabbed his, put a piece of torrone on his palm, and closed his fingers tight. Nicola felt Maria's strength crushing his knuckles, and he was afraid, he would stain his cuffs, he wasn't a child who spilled his food, he knew how to eat properly, neatly. Then, conscious and lucid, he noticed hunger. How sweet, in memory, was the taste of the hot chocolate under Maria's attentive gaze, how he would have liked to place his mouth on that blue and white porcelain cup, smell Caffè Spinelli's odor of smoke and bergamot. He lay down near the basin, straightened his back, and on all fours leaned over the edge and licked it. He went on for hours and hours, drinking and licking in measured mouthfuls, and soaking his pants, sometimes watchful, sometimes enveloped in a distorted sleep. Abrupt, trancelike sleeps and sudden reawakenings were his nights and his dawns, in that undefined time without nights or dawns. Minutes, hours, days became confused in an impossible calendar.

Finally, a known voice vibrated in the silence. "Here! Here!" he shouted and a man replied no, only dead there, pointless to insist, in that building no one had survived.

"Dig here, please," she begged, again, and to Nicola she seemed desperate.

"Madame!" he screamed, and cursed himself for having wept and shouted when there was no one, now that he needed words.

"Did you hear?" she wept, and the child called again and again.

"Madame, I'm here! In the cellar!" and his lifeline was the Frenchwoman's tears and the sounds approaching the trapdoor.

"Open it! Open it! There's an iron handle!" Nicola gave instructions while Madame's tone became assertive, persuasive, calmed him, begged him to hold on, and other hands were digging, faster and faster.

When the trapdoor opened, Nicola came out into the reddish

light of sunset, and Madame was sitting on a pile of rubble, huddled in a man's coat.

"Look how cute this *picciriddu*," she was moved, and hugged
him. "I won't leave you, I'll take you with me."

"Let's go, signora!" one of the two men urged her, but she gave
Nicola a caring look.

"I'll take him with me," she insisted.

"It's the third time you've said it, you can't take them all, we've
already explained to you," said one.

"Signora," the other joined in, "it's better if you don't stop, we'll
save more of them. We have too many, still underground. This
one will manage, he's big." Then, to Nicola: "Run to the harbor,
there are priests who are rounding up the children of the area,
they'll give you food, they'll take care of you."

Madame grew sad and loosened her grip on the child.

"No, if you can you should sail away, any place will be safe, go
far away from here."

"Where's my mother?" the child asked. "And why can't I come
with you?"

"The signora is helping us uncover others like you. She divines
where they're alive, there are so many of you underground, she
indicates to us where to dig."

It was then that Nicola looked around and truly saw what
remained of his life. Of the building where he was born and grew
up, only the arch that separated the dining room from the entrance
was standing, without walls or ceilings. The rest was dust, stones,
the ruined outline of his mother's night table, the dishes shards
with white and yellow flowers, books crushed by bricks, shattered
furniture, splinters of mirrors. A giant had sat on the house, and it
had been unable to bear the weight.

"You remember me? I came with my mother! My mother,

Maria, the blonde with a Veneto accent! You picked a card and the Devil came out!"

Madame nodded wearily. She didn't seem interested in memories.

"Listen to me, go to the harbor, escape: there's nothing left here, and the earth is still shaking," she insisted. "Escape to safety."

Madame was persuasive, and yet Nicola couldn't tear himself away if there was even just a hope of finding Maria alive under the ruins.

"At least tell me, is my mother dead? You know everything, is my mother alive or dead?"

"Did she live here, your mother? With you? She slept in the bed with your father?"

Nicola nodded.

"There's no one left in this square. I heard only you."

"Dig there! They slept on this side of the house," Nicola implored.

"We can take him part of the way, the next house we have to visit is before the Marina," one of the two men proposed, seeing that Madame was hesitating.

They all four set off toward the sea, the two men in front and the Frenchwoman leading the child.

"Do you remember when I came to you with my mother? And you said that the devils would come and get me?"

"I didn't say that."

"There was a devil with two helpers."

Madame squeezed his knuckles tighter.

"As you see, they didn't come and get you."

Nicola's palm slipped out of the woman's grip.

"What do you mean? I have to save my mother! It's up to me to save my mother from Hell!" he had begun to shout, looking around like a frightened animal. "I'm not going anywhere with you! I have to save my mother! She's alive! She's always protected me! It's because of her that I'm alive!"

"Believe me, go to the harbor, get away from that house, there's no one there," Madame tried in vain to restrain him, but Nicola wriggled away and his cries attracted attention. "What's wrong with that child? What are you doing to him?" The last thing Nicola heard was a woman approaching, while the two men urged Madame not to waste time. Then everything dissolved behind him as he ran among the ruins to return to his cellar, to his mother.

Reaching what was left of the house, he began digging. Mamma, Mamma, he sobbed. He couldn't go anywhere without her, regret would follow: she had protected him and he had abandoned her. He didn't trust the words of the Frenchwoman, what did she know about his mother? He didn't believe her, he believed only in the love of Maria, the only love he had known. Mamma, he sobbed again, until from the ruins a wrought-iron foot emerged, a foot with a ridged base, his parents' bed. He wept harder, he was right: they were there and were waiting for him. He kept digging until he touched something that wasn't metal and wasn't stone and he grabbed it, he felt a prickly fabric and from the cuff he recognized the yellow garment Maria slept in, from which four of his mother's fingers emerged. Nicola retreated, horrified.

"My mother, here! My mother's here!" he shouted, but no one was around.

New roars broke the silence. Other pieces of the house fell, and a mountain of splinters and masonry buried Maria's body forever. Nicola dodged a rain of pebbles on his head and forehead. If he stayed there he would be dead. He, too.

# THE TOWER

*He who builds a "tower" to replace revelation from heaven by what he himself has fabricated, will be blasted by a thunderbolt, i.e. he will undergo the humiliation of being reduced to his own subjectivity and to terrestrial reality.*

At five-twenty-one, in Messina, my desire and goal, my origin and chosen destiny, capital and antithesis of the village I was escaping, the living no longer existed. Only the dead and the living dead.

I, fallen like a sinner angel—to which category did I belong?

Bruised but whole, for long minutes in my ears I heard the echo of thunder spit out by the abyss, in my eyes smoke and ashes, under my body a dough of concrete and, above, a rain of fog. The waves that wanted to consume me retreated.

Then silence.

The girl who came down with the façade of her apartment was me. The girl carried away from the window, hurtled from a wretched third floor onto a pile of rubble, had my face, my skin. That mound with its grotesque welcome, that mound of walls and objects that had been my life, had saved my body—under me might be tables and curtains, wardrobes and human beings.

Behind an elsewhere of fallen walls the prayer rose distinctly: *Arcangelu Micheli, si è pi' mali 'nesci beni*, what has come to bring me harm, let it turn instead to good. It was the prayer Grandmother and I recited when I was little, the formula invoked to drive out the evil beings that nightmares put in my bed. With that prayer, Grandmother spoke to the dreams that were dreams and the real that was real, baptized and separated truth from illusion. The exorcism didn't work this time. Out of the hill of rubble from which it had risen, the voice stopped existing and my grandmother with it. I shouted her name, her bare name the same as mine, as if calling a different me, and I ran to dig at the point where I was sure I'd heard her, until two warm hands circled my hips and pulled me away an instant before a beam fell. Only then I understood that what had happened had happened to me.

The earth shook again, pulverized other beams, other columns. Snatching me from my grandmother's tomb before it became mine was, I recognized, the neighbor, the mother of three girls—she was digging with hands and feet, careless of the nakedness her nightgown exposed. I myself must have appeared lewd, my legs were cold, was it a sign that I was alive? What would happen if men saw me?

The neighbor's daughters were beneath us, but I heard no voices, heard no sound.

An evil fog obstructed my sight.

I lay down, curled up on one side, and wept. My cheeks pressed against the cold ruins, and the tears fell on what remained of my existence. In a rage I began biting and scratching pieces of floor and walls, I looked up and above me saw emerging through the smoke shreds of the façade, windows open onto nothing.

The walls shook. I ran a few meters farther on, and, finally finding the courage to look, saw what remained of the building: a lopped and imploded line. Grandmother and I used to call it *'a muragghia*, the great wall, because once when I was little we had read an Oriental fable set at the foot of a very long wall, a huge wall, in fact, which in ancient times had served to isolate and fortify China. In the same way, our Palazzata, which, with its endless wall of apartments and offices, looked over the Strait, seemed to protect the city from disasters threatened by the sea: but that, too, was only an illusion.

The woman who had been our neighbor came over to me. She, like me, was weeping, she covered her face with her hands. Her magnificent curly hair, which I remembered as well brushed and soft, lay wiry and wild on her shoulders, while she shook and sobbed. I tried to embrace her.

"I kissed all the children," she said, staring at me, as if entreating me. "All three, before I went to bed, all three, Isabella, Ada, Lina, I called them, all three, and they answered, the little one never wanted to close her eyes, you know? She was always the last to fall asleep, because I like that I still see you, Mamma, she'd say. You don't have children, I envy you, because right now I'd like someone to rip my heart out."

"They'll come and help you, I swear," I lied.

A short distance from us a chest was sticking out of the rubble, I went over and took everything I found, cloaks, dresses, I filled my arms and showed the booty to the woman, so that we could both cover ourselves, wear something over our nightgowns. She put on a coat and didn't want anything else, I tied the rest up in a bundle, using a shawl, I would think about it later. It seemed to me more important to take care of her, it was the way to put off reckoning with my terror and my losses.

"I bore them. I carried all three in my belly," she said, eyes staring into a void. From now on she would have to live without pieces of her own body, stripped of something I had never known, and so I couldn't feel the lack.

I had no words for her grief, which overwhelmed me, swallowing mine. I introduced myself and asked her name, I knew only the surname of her husband.

"My name is Elvira," she said.

I covered myself as well as I could while day rose to illuminate the devastation of everything and our nothing.

The earth shook again, yet another piece of the house fell. Instinctively we hugged each other.

"Let's go, let's look for a safer place," I said to Elvira. "There must be a safer place, let's go to the sea."

"My little ones are here!" she cried, and then: "Go, I want to die with them."

She had her daughters and I had only her, a woman with whom I had never before spoken, but our houses had collapsed together. I didn't go.

Voices and faces arrived soon afterward, when, with the lights of morning, a dark, swarming movement began.

Men and women advanced amid the ruins, clasping hands in recognition or even just in trust, seeking contact, acknowledgment. A young woman dressed in white passed, a group of boys with a priest, an old man hurrying toward the harbor. Elvira threw herself at him, imploring him to dig up her children, he glared at her and shook her off. All those people were desperate as she was, as we were, we were walking over the dead, in the midst of the dead, still without truly understanding that we were alive, unsure whether we really were. Each of us can focus more easily on a circumscribed suffering than on too much suffering at once, so Elvira's trouble became mine; seeing her beg like that caused me pain and a voice within suggested, rest, your daughters no longer exist, save the suffering for your future life. I begged her to wait, her husband and children would make it, I don't know why I told that lie, but then I understood that we would have to live on lies forever. Elvira gave a mean laugh, she said her husband was safe, he hadn't come home, in order to sleep at his lover's, didn't I know men? Of course, you don't know anything, you who aren't married.

I didn't answer. There was too much despair everywhere, there was no room in me to take in meanness. I left Elvira and began to hang around the Palazzata and the fires that were turning it red, I counted the non-dead without daring to call them living, and among them, in confusion, I tried to identify myself. If I was no longer I, maybe I could look for a place in an us? I looked, powerless, letting visions and thoughts flow. Us, silhouettes without edges in clouds of fiery smoke and debris, unable to focus even our consciousness, we struggled to discover whether a limb still responded or not, whether we still had a bone, we tried to move legs buried by kilos of bricks, to dig arms out from under furniture, remove from our nose, our forehead, the remains of dwellings and things that were ours and old. We hung from cornices and balconies, contracting muscles we didn't even know we had, asked and gave credence to sounds that indicated below or above us the breath of another person. We wept because what those who had lost everything had was not life, and at every instant we knew we were still losing something, someone, in the holes and hollows where a voice rose and after a moment was gone.

Gradually, as sections of the Palazzata continued to crumble, it lost its linearity. Neither the streets nor the squares were the known ones, my sense of direction was useless. When I saw the white hem of Elvira's nightgown sticking out from under a dark overcoat, I realized I had returned to the point of departure.

Two men in police uniforms arrived and attended to her, as she wept ceaselessly for her daughters. They said the priority was to search for children, they listened to her, but one of the two was staring at her breasts, and it seemed to me that he was not to be trusted; I tried to go to her aid, but she resisted violently, pushing me aside, and went on talking to them. I gave up, no one could decide for someone else what was right to do. What had been my dearest wish until the day before, to be free—well, it had been granted. Maybe Elvira was right, in me relief balanced grief, I would no longer hear my grandmother's reproach, I would not have to ask permission for my ambitions, apologize for my behavior. Of course, I would never have suspected that freedom would be presented to me in the guise of an abyss: so little do we know about the shape of the future and the substance of desires that it's best not to linger there too long. The hope I had lived on until then appeared in its troubling truth: it had been only one version of my collapse, I was free in a frightening and irreversible way, and I had to use that gift before it used me. There wasn't time, "time" was a mesmerizing and dying word, and day broke in spite of everything: maybe it would rain and we would all be without shelter. That's what I needed, shelter, while the crackling wires of the devastated tram line created a ridiculous effect like footlights.

I retreated behind a standing wall, where I took off my nightgown and put on the stolen clothes. Which of my neighbors did the warm and elegant red wool camisole I put on belong to, and that incongruous lace shawl I wrapped around my head: I half-closed my eyelids and the women of the Palazzata paraded before me, the brunette with slender legs, the redhead with the long nose and kind expression, the hateful one who looked at me disdain-fully, and the others I would not see again. A cornice fell on a stove and a pile of crumbled wall exploded nearby. I escaped from the smoke, leaving behind the clothes I hadn't put on, and gave up the idea of hiding them and retrieving them later. With an out of place elegance masking swollen eyes and bare feet, I set off through the city, and only then did there begin to be room for other thoughts.

My father, I wondered, was he alive or dead?

Had the end of the world struck him, too, or spared him?

I heard his voice in my ears as he made his way through the rubble and came toward me murmuring: Rina, Rina.

I hated that name, and yet in spite of myself I longed for it madly, it would have made me feel safe, as we're safe in what's keeping us in prison, and when the prison opens we are left unprotected.

But no, I wasn't Rina, I was Barbara: in Messina and forever. My father's principal effort had been to hinder every kind of hap-piness in order to sacrifice me to a distorted idea of safety. And yet it wasn't he who had saved me but the city that he wished to keep me from, and that even while it collapsed and died had spared me. Rina, Rina: I would never respond to the diminutive, only to my full name and with no added surnames.

Barefoot, I walked through the ruins of the city my father had rejected and I had never stopped believing in; every scrap, every place or thing he despised or didn't know had been for me a source of interest. All my life I had looked where he wouldn't look, wished to walk along streets that he avoided, and yet now that my bare feet were treading the dust, and the devastations wounding my ankles, I wished for the shell and protection of his shoes. Strong shoes, charmless work shoes, shoes that my grandmother looked at with despair because they were the symbol of that renunciation of urbanity that she couldn't understand or tolerate: if only I had been able to dig up a similar pair, belonging to a man like him, then my progress would have been different. Instead I advanced hesitantly in the ghost city, I myself became a ghost, and Messina was a putrescent body, a large mouth with rotten smoky breath. Every corner stank of the dead, of broken aqueducts, of food spewed out of pantries that had no master, yet I continued my pilgrimage toward the cathedral, sure that it had remained standing, and that the good people would have found shelter there; the wish to kneel before the altar and pray for my buried world impelled me to go forward without stopping. Every so often, in the groups of wanderers, I could distinguish faces of people I had perhaps encountered, but I was never certain—I didn't know many people in Messina. The buildings, those yes, I knew them perfectly, friezes and doorways that populated my solitary walks stood out clearly in my memory, although in the outside world they no longer existed: in vain I sought them in empty spaces and gaps.

No longer aligned, undamaged houses and destroyed ones alternated without sense or reason; some had been spared and others flattened according to mysterious designs of fate and urban planning. That night, God had sat at a gaming table, one of many set up for the Christmas celebrations; he had won and lost, had drunk toasts and got angry, had thrown down in no order everything within reach.

I was relieved to see a corner of the façade of the Vittorio Emanuele: the theater where just a few hours before I'd seen *Aida* had been saved, I rejoiced. I thought of Vittorio, of his emerald eyes, which I felt had observed me in a way unknown in my family; tears rose and I had to stop, and suddenly I felt a new warmth.

The heat worked its way between my ankles, and a cry roused me: the fur of a kitten rubbing against my feet, under the skirt. I caressed it, the first living animal I'd met since the world collapsed. It studied me sadly; once it understood that I had nothing to feed it, it went away.

The souls of the dogs, cats, birds, and all the other dead animals, swept away by the water from the streams and consumed by the sea, would continue to live with those of the human beings.

I forced myself to start walking again. At the theater I would find someone. I had the illusion that the magic of the past evening had held up the entire building, as if nothing had happened.

The light of that false confidence faded as I approached: little more than the theater's façade remained, as in performances of plays that had been staged there. The entire city was a wing in the theater, the faces of buildings endured, concealing behind their backs ripped-out beams, broken furniture, crippled armoires and beds; the outsides were plaques behind which tombs and bones were mixed, as in the cemetery. Messina, a dying body, was bleeding from shattered windows and, despite the bleeding, wouldn't die but endured, stinking of discomfort and manure. In front of the Duomo I gave up. In what religion would its fate have been different?

Only the door of the cathedral was left, miraculously spared beneath the façade that had crumpled and fallen on itself, its fragments scattered over the pavement of Sundays. Splinters of the façade had ended up in the stagnant water of the Fountain of Orion; every so often the sun was obscured and brief, muggy discharges of rain came down, which didn't put out the fires but soaked my clothes.

Not far away a mound was burning. I was afraid of those fires, which ignited out of nothing in the rubble, I moved away and headed toward Piazza Pantadattilo. If houses and churches were mostly destroyed, fountains and statues survived in the inferno with an audacity that made them seem proud or merciful, according to whether they looked up or down, talked with God or were moved to pity us mortals.

The tall statue of the Madonna Immacolata aimed at the sky with disconsolate eyes and hands in prayer; the *putti* under her no longer seemed satisfied, happy children but small, lost, imploring angels. One of the Virgin's feet trampled a serpent and the other rested on a crescent moon. I clung to that vision with my last strength: the night star under Maria's left heel replaced the altar buried under the ruins of the cathedral. I knelt to that trampled moon and addressed to it my liturgy.

# THE CHARIOT

*Be that as it may, the charioteer of the Arcanum "The*
*Chariot" is the victor over trials, i.e. the temptations,*
*and if he is master, then it is thanks to himself. He*
*is alone, standing in his chariot; no one is present*
*to applaud him or to pay homage to him; he has*
*no weapons—the sceptre that he holds not being a*
*weapon. If he is master, his mastership was acquired*
*in solitude and he owes it to the trials alone, and not*
*to anyone or anything external to himself.*

Maybe the problem was names.

He had to find other ones, cancel the old titles of things and
places, rewrite the dictionary and the geography book, think
up and print as soon as possible a map with a new set of names.
Maybe what at one time was for Nicola "home" would have a less
frightening aspect if from now on he called it something different.
Maybe, maybe, maybe: the ideas arrived insecurely and skewed,
attempts rather than certainties, superimpositions of memory on
the gaze, and the two things never came together. The memory
was always excessive or deficient: where before there had been a

church now there was nothing, where there had been nothing were ruins. The road to the port was a hurdle in a disconnected present. On the way one encountered only creatures who, like Nicola, were walking toward the sea carrying a few clothes, small bags. Among them he recognized Dalila, a dark, shapely woman who had married an employee of Vincenzo's. Every so often she and her husband came to dinner at the Fera house; they didn't have children and made vulgar comments about children and the couples who had them, but Nicola's parents were permissive with them, laughing at remarks they would not have forgiven in others. On those nights he didn't exist, but when he had to go to bed Maria, too, rose from the table: Excuse me, but if I don't go with him he won't sleep, my son can't do anything without me. The illusion of not existing ended as usual with the ropes tight around his wrists, pulling him down into night, while above his head the adults' din was slow to end. But Dalila was alive and Maria was no longer there. Nicola went up to her as if to cling to that last residue of mother.

"Do you have anything to eat?" he implored. She reacted as if a bloodsucker had attacked her arm.

"You're the only one of your family saved?"

Nicola nodded, and the woman said to her group: "You who doubt the devil, do you want another proof? You remember the Fera bergamot, that very honest Vincenzo and his wonderful small, shy wife from the continent? In the house they had a nightmare, a creature from the inferno, the poor woman used to help her husband, then she had to give it up to stay with him. What do you want, she was good, she wouldn't leave the child." And, almost screaming: "She told me he was possessed by the Devil. She lost sleep and money because she loved him more than her life, with the new year an expert priest was supposed to come from Cosenza to do an exorcism, but see what an end they came to?"

Nicola was paralyzed.

"And out of the whole family who survived? Those who carried high the name of Reggio throughout Italy are no longer here, and the *picciriddu* sent by the devil is alive!"

A man with a mustache approached Nicola. "Did you take your father's money, too? Let's see." He moved to stick his hands in Nicola's pockets. Nicola fled and the man chased him. Only after climbing over ruins and dodging fires, after leaving behind agitated voices that shouted at him that the earthquake was his fault, his, that he would have to die to free them from the evil eye, after fearing that his head and lungs would go along with his breath, that Dalila's friends would shoot him or that he would stumble and die incinerated, was Nicola able to slip through an open doorway. Not even then did he feel safe, but his breath slowed and his blood began flowing. He spat on the ground and decided to go in, even if nothing appeared really secure, neither roof nor walls. He might as well die in a collapse, and in a moment he was at the top of the stairs, but the floor above no longer existed, the steps led nowhere, he was forced to come down. He entered one of the rooms on the ground floor, an undamaged living room where there was a couch, upholstered chairs, a sideboard with decorated glass. On a small low table a tray of oranges and cookies appeared: Nicola pounced on the food and began stuffing himself. The more he ate the more upset his stomach was, he ate with primitive hunger, as if he were consuming the last meal on Earth, he ate until nausea stopped him, and he was still eating when the first waves of vomiting arrived with the smell of citrus. After he threw up he was more lucid, and he cleaned himself off with the napkin that covered the basket. He opened the drawers of the sideboard and found the silverware. He took the cover off a pillow and, with that material, made a bag, stuck in it every piece of silver he could grab, and stuffed cookies in his pockets until they were reduced to a mush. One more look at the apartment and he was off, running toward the port.

Amid the fumes of excrement rose an unmistakable odor of salt. The Strait, in spite of everything, still existed. Suddenly in the distance he saw the silhouette of Dalila again, as if she were about to enter a theater, Nicola stopped. He wasn't afraid so much of her as of the men who were with her; they were hefty men and could hurt him, so he scratched his back against a wall as he waited to decide the best move, and when he heard steps he turned, frightened.

"Are you alone?" asked a man in a torn shirt and sagging pants. Nicola shook his head no. "Where are your mother and father?"

He wasn't ready for that question. He thought no one would ask it, now that everyone was dead, and he needed an excuse, any kind, to keep the man from thinking he had no one, from hurting him. What was the quickest, the likeliest? They had gone in search of a boat to carry them all to safety? To pee, to recover a precious object under the ruins. They were around the corner, right there, they were about to arrive. They were at home, but they would be here soon. So, what could he invent about his parents?

"I'm alone, too. I had a wife and four children, the oldest like you. Twelve?"

"Eleven."

"His name was Marco. Marco Giuseppe, the name of an uncle of my wife, Carla, and of my cousin who died at sea. Names are important. They're all that remains to us."

So adults also wept. Nicola had never seen an adult so shattered.

"What's your name?"

"Nicola Vincenzo Maria Fera. My name, the name of my father, the name of my mother and the Madonna."

"Fera? Like the perfume?"

"My father invented it."

"You were rich, then. I had nothing. In reality I had everything and didn't realize it, I was desperate because I wasn't always able to feed my children. The boat wasn't enough, some days the sea was really *schifusazzu*, disgusting."

Nicola lowered his gaze, mortified, though that wealth that took away from others wasn't his fault or his family's.

"The waves consumed the boat before my eyes, and the earth the house behind me. I was in the middle and was saved. Unfortunately."

Nicola opened the bag he'd made from the pillowcase and showed the fisherman the silver taken from the house that had collapsed.

"Take it, I have a lot. Take it."

The man didn't seem interested. "The world is over. You have all life ahead, you shouldn't stay here with us. At the port there's a line for the ships. Bye, Marco. Marco Giuseppe. Save yourself."

The fisherman began weeping again: that meeting seemed to have been only a parenthesis between old tears and new. He was the first adult Nicola hadn't had to protect himself from and, under the influence of an uncertain form of gratitude, he felt a desire to embrace him. He pulled out a handful of cookies and put them in the man's hands along with a silver spoon. Then the earth shook again, lightly, and, while the jolt made his feet dance, the child resumed his journey.

When he was able to see the entire Strait, it appeared in its cruel majesty, the waters here black, there faded, elsewhere still of an intense blue, indifferent to the disaster.

And so Nicola reached the port, yet another name to change. That place had been life and movement, festive and bustling, but now it was a catacomb: relics of departures could be imagined in the depths, steamships and sailboats struck and sent flying, while the uprooted buoys had swum toward land or the open sea. Muddy tangles of carts, barrels, wheels, bits of houses, bannisters, fragments of boats dragged by the mad waves had been rolled onto the pier, jolts of land and water had gone wild creating gaps and cracks in the street. In place of the Marina, with its two broad straight roads to the north and the south, twisting paths originated amid the wreckage. The fountain that ornamented the road along the sea had been swept away, like the bathhouses on stilts beloved of swimmers. The beach where Nicola would have liked to learn to swim and Maria had never taken him had disappeared; near the bathhouse was an open space bigger than others, and a group of men were lining up bodies in piles, some covered with water, some with lime. Urban dust buried life.

"Messina is worse than Reggio, why would you go to Messina?"

A sailor tried to hold back the crowd of people who wanted to get in his torpedo boat, while colleagues distributed food and water before setting off.

"Go get the train! To Naples, to Italy!"

In the crowd, fragments of conversation, varying between men and women, impossible to catch more than a few words in a row, a reasonable sentence, track who said what. There's a train leaving for Naples . . . They won't let us get on . . . They want to kill us all . . . They've given orders to bomb the city . . . I have a cousin in Cannitello . . . Do you have any news of my husband . . . The railroad was demolished . . . There are no tracks . . . Messina is burning . . . Summon the king! Summon the Pope! . . . Do you have a little water for me . . .

People were heading toward the station, the sailors had been immovable. Among those who turned their back on the sea to hurry to the station was Dalila; her gait had changed, now she rudely took off and left her companions behind, shoving anyone who got in her way, as if only she had to be saved. Nicola waited until he couldn't see her anymore. Finally, when he was sure he was alone, he turned to the sailor.

"Can I come with you?"

"You don't have anyone to go and take the train with you?"

"They told me to go to the port and get on a ship."

"Sicily is destroyed. We're going to Messina to bring aid to people who are worse off than here—what do you want? Do you have someone to take care of you?"

"An aunt," Nicola lied. He couldn't risk either wasting more time or taking the same train as the woman who had incited those terrifying men against him. He had to get on that boat at any cost, and Messina was the only city he knew, apart from his own.

The sailor wasn't convinced, but Nicola wouldn't move.

"It's not just my mother's sister, there's her family, too. My cousins, aunts and uncles, someone must have survived, they all love me, they'll be worried, maybe they'll want to come, better for me to go right away."

Seeing that words were not enough, he took two pieces of silverware out of his sack.

"Get in," the sailor ordered, looking around, but without taking them.

Standing on the bridge of the torpedo boat *Morgana*, Nicola crossed a dark, delirious Strait in silence. From the sea loomed the spectacle of Messina in ashes. At Capo Peloro, the lighthouse tower appeared split, as if a giant had struck it with an axe, the metal bent and twisted in the form of a serpent. Of the low, cheerful habitations of the villages on the shore solitary walls remained, among the white walls the frescoed ones indicated that there had been a church: even the houses of God had come down.

The Palazzata was a toothless jaw breathing smoke, sometimes red from the flames. Only the Hills of Neptune, with their radiant green woods, seemed to have been spared by death.

A little before landing, the sailor showed up again.

"What neighborhood does your aunt live in?"

"In the Palazzata," Nicola answered quickly, fearful that if he mentioned a more distant area the man would offer to go with him.

The sailor stared at him. He looked at his shiny leather shoes, his refined clothes.

"Is she wealthy like you?"

Nicola understood immediately where he wanted to strike.

"I don't think those objects you have there will be of use to her. But I have to work for a living—I could die saving the children, buried by another aftershock."

Only after handing over to that man the bag with the silver that he had taken with him for the days to come, Nicola descended from the torpedo boat *Morgana* and touched island soil.

# JUSTICE

*It is the balance which indicates equilibrium—or order, health, harmony and justice—and it is the sword which signifies the power to re-establish it each time that the individual will sins against the universal will.*

While I was kneeling at the feet of the Madonna and the moon, another woman knelt beside me; her head was covered, her fingers intertwined and scratched, and she wept and prayed noisily. Her smell distracted me: it was a long time since I'd smelled someone's skin so close up without perfumes or artifices. She'd been sweating, and everything about her was sour and damp; on the backs of her hands tears mingled with drops of that liquid with which her body rejected the earthquake's attack.

I broke off my prayer and waited until she finished hers, and then we began talking immediately, needing no excuse, saying to each other that the Madonna would intercede for us. As if I had known her forever, I told her about my father and my grandmother, I confessed that in the midst of the horror an unexpected faith in the days to come was emerging in me, because I would be able to invent myself. I was ashamed of that thought, but since I wouldn't see her again, and she was a stranger, she wouldn't judge me. And you, I asked in return, you have no one?

She said that years ago she had made the best possible marriage, because she had married the Lord. So I had just told a nun that my sorrow wasn't pure, but mixed with an inadmissible relief. I retreated in shame, and also to observe her carefully: she wasn't wearing her habit, since she, too, had been caught sleeping, and there was nothing that would have revealed her situation.

Her name was Rosalba, and she was a novice at the monastery of Santa Teresa; many of the sisters were still buried, and the others continued to dig, while they settled themselves as well as they could in the garden, constructing out of the rubble some small emergency caves. I felt tenderness for those women who had chosen to live in seclusion, far from the human gaze, serving and praising God, until he decided to destroy the shell and expose them to the eyes of the world.

Rosalba told me that already since late morning neighbors who were fleeing to the port or the station had been giving them provisions; she asked if I had eaten, if I had a place to spend the night, I said no to both, and, as we went on talking, I followed her to the convent, or what remained of it. We were greeted by the shouts of a girl Rosalba recognized, and she quickened her pace. Thus, even before introducing myself, I helped the sisters get a novice out of a hole; she refused to emerge naked, so I threw on her a blue dress with a higher neck than the others, choosing it from among the garments piled up in the middle of the garden.

A large quantity of clothes that no one would have found worthy of giving me had been donated to the nuns: people had taken care to cover their own bodies, and even those without life took precedence over ours. But the sisters made no distinction between me and them, and invited me to take what I wanted from an excess of corsets, cloaks, and blankets. I filled a bag with some changes of clothes, and found a pair of shoes in my size, white and decorated, summer shoes but with strong soles. I ate something with the sisters, then curled up on the pallet they offered me and, finally, protected by those women, allowed myself to sleep.

At dawn, my feet armored against the shards and spikes of a treacherous earth, I wanted to resume wandering through Messina. In fact I hadn't slept more than a couple of hours, disturbed by *Aida*, which continued to be staged intermittently in my head: the charcoal-covered faces of the actors faded to show their frightening identities; deformed features startled me awake. My father had also appeared as I slept: blurry but unmistakable, he was walking along a platform at the station in Scaletta Zanclea calling me by my nickname, Rina, Rina, and snarling at me, until a roar buried his reproaches, leaving me in doubt whether he was real or not, because from time to time the earth shook. As time passed, apprehension about seeing my father was transformed into fear that I would see him. I fought against that feeling, against that sin: the prohibitions he had brought me up with were disintegrating like the buildings of Messina, but deep down I had no desire for those prohibitions to be standing again, as I had for the buildings. Between revelations and memories, the cat had re-emerged between my ankles; I had felt on me my grandmother's wrinkled hands, mottled and familiar, and had transfigured the faces of the sisters beside me. The reality, although frightening, was less so than dreams: sleeping I was powerless and had to endure everything; awake, I could live and react. If there was a light in the darkness, that light came with the day.

At dawn on December 29th, Messina was an open scar. The night before, the nuns had shared with me cheese and dried figs from a barrel in which they had packed the provisions that neighbors, priests, and passersby had scraped together for them. They were setting up a temporary camp where they could all stay together before being reassigned to other convents; they wanted to help as much as possible, feeling that it was right not to leave immediately, to remain within the wound of the city that housed them, to heal it. I wasn't full and yet I didn't feel hungry, I was only thirsty, and a rumor spread that at the Marina the people bringing aid were distributing water to the evacuees. That was what they called us: evacuees. We still didn't know who we were, we had just begun to admit we were alive, and already we had become a problem.

I decided to go. I wanted to get some water and offer a prayer at Grandmother Barbara's tomb, kneel and ask forgiveness for her death, which weighed on me even if I hadn't caused it. During the night, crosses had emerged on the mounds of crumbled buildings and among the piles of bodies, improvised with pieces of wood and iron, or contrived from metal plates and pipes; wherever there were two sticks, there were people to make a cross and plant it, marking a grave. At times I saw the cross and didn't see the bodies: beneath it someone had left a family and every hope of recovery.

Nothing was whole in the landscape, apart from the neighborhood of Tirone, a street lined by low stone houses set in the green and the rock, which insisted on happily winding over the hills. I lacked the courage to venture there, I envied the families that hadn't lost anyone. On the hilltops, scattered over various points of the city, the statues towered, all spared by the earthquake, suddenly mocking us. Bold Neptune turned his solid buttocks to the sea, his fleshy calves, the long sensual back; with his right hand he pointed to Messina, blessing it with pagan indulgence, in his left he grasped the trident. In the middle of his square Don Giovanni of Austria, victorious after the battle of Lepanto, still trampled the severed head of a Turkish commander, but the earthquake had inverted the meaning of the scene and the role of the subjects: until two days before, the commander had emanated glory and power; now he had the threatening expression of a punisher. We no longer rejoiced with him; rather, we identified with the adversary, each of us transformed, crushed by an obscure and violent enemy. The image was disturbing, but I also felt a great force within me, the force of those who have to repair and repair themselves, walk without yielding to any distraction, ever. For a girl alone, wandering through apocalyptic Messina meant a constant vigilance, holding on to the fear that someone was following, could terrify you at any moment. It meant being ready to camouflage yourself in a group of strangers, pretending to be one of them if a shifty look lingered on your solitude; run away if a mound of debris started burning; stay out of quarrels; keep away from those clutching a knife in their pocket or a pistol stolen from the ruins of armories and knife shops. In that situation anyone could become a criminal, all the more unrestrainable because he wasn't accustomed to weapons and hadn't mastered their use. Walking alone meant keeping calm when someone shouted that all the inmates had escaped from the jail and the psychiatric hospital, that there were assaults on the safes in banks and the customs-house stores. It meant knowing that in the uncontrolled city one could choose a single way: survive at all costs. More than by hunger, filth, fear, greed, and emotion, people were driven by thirst, because pipes and aqueducts were broken and unusable; some went around with bottles full of sea water, but mainly we drank from puddles, putting into our bodies the putrid water of latrines and ruptured sewers, of burst tanks, rivulets that had carried away the corpses of our families and the rubble of our houses.

Gradually as I approached the Marina I encountered foreign

sailors in light-colored uniforms, berets and badges, tall boots. They spoke among themselves an alarmed language, bristling with accents but slippery, rapid, that gave me an unwanted joy. A girl in a gray nightgown, wide sleeves gathered at the wrists, followed one of them, who was tall and robust, with a pale face, pointing out to him a nearby house; she shouted and begged him in dialect to go and save her brother, he was still speaking, she could hear him under the ruins. The soldier stopped, called to a colleague, and together they followed her; I, too, followed, at a little distance, to make sure nothing bad happened to that creature with the anguished face; then I saw the mother, on a mass of ruins that must have been the tomb of her son, so distraught she couldn't look anyone in the face, and I stayed to watch them both, under the illusion that I was protecting them.

After ten minutes, the sailors pulled out a small foot, a small leg, finally a child, whole and alive. The mother watched the scene as if her son were coming into the world for the second time, and as his small body emerged from the hole her weeping grew even louder. The sailors said something else, the mother asked where they were from, and this time they understood her: Russia, Russia. Then they rejoined their group, the woman followed them shouting thanks in dialect, but they answered only *nichevo*, *nichevo*. I liked the sound of that word, *nichevo*, I memorized it as I continued on my way, and again approached that great theater where the Palazzata had been, with its connecting gates between the sea and the city, its shops and offices, our houses, the town hall, the maritime health office, the marine navigation company. Over their ashes human beings moved in packs, the women covered by dressing gowns and with big bundles on their heads, the men dragging sacks and bags. There was another woman alone like me, one of the few not wearing black, in her thirties, in a tight-fitting light green top. When I passed by she called to me, and I was surprised that she knew my name.

"You're the widow Ruello's granddaughter," she explained, seeing my surprise. "You and your grandmother are very similar-looking." At that word "grandmother" I couldn't not stop.

Jutta was Bavarian. She had been traveling in Sicily for several days and through Europe for more than a month, and had come to Messina for New Year's. Ten years earlier, she said, she and her husband had lived in Italy. They were marine biologists who studied the sea floor and had done research on the flora and fauna of the Strait. Her husband had died suddenly, of a heart attack, in the summer, and she had had a desire to visit all the places where they had been happy.

"Did you travel alone?" I asked, admiring of that initiative, and Jutta said no, she had left with a friend and a maid, but she had no news of either of them. The rooms of the Grand Hotel Trinacria had collapsed, she had been saved because the pillar at the head of her bed stayed fixed while the rest fell; but her back hurt and she was bruised all over, she couldn't walk without pain. I asked if she had eaten, she said the Russian sailors had given her some dried cod, there were barrels of it at the port and the customs house, but unfortunately that salty food had merely increased her thirst. I promised that as soon as I found some water I would return and share it with her.

"I was also at the theater for *Aida*," she continued before saying goodbye. "What a magical evening, and how beautiful you were. I would have liked to meet you, but you seemed sad and angry, and I just had time to greet your grandmother." Again that word acted in me like a magic formula: it was all that would remain to me of her, her inheritance, my future. Grandmother. I was curious to know their relations, but my throat was so dry I couldn't speak, I couldn't hold out a minute more, I would have done anything for a drop of water. An Italian torpedo boat that surely brought some sort of aid had docked, and I hurried to get in line. Somewhere else people were shouting, Look, the king! look, the queen! But I was too thirsty, I could barely stand up with that burning thirst.

I got ready to plead with the soldiers, and I was very surprised when I saw a well-dressed child of scarcely twelve disembark. No adult followed him, he carried nothing, and he looked around as if he had just arrived from the moon.

# DEATH

*Our empirical experience of death is the disappearance from the physical plane of living beings. Such is the fact of our experience from without, that we have by means of our five senses. But the disappearance as such is not confined to the domain of outward experience of the senses. It is experienced also in the domain of inner experience, in that of consciousness. There the images and representations disappear just as living beings do so for the experience of the senses. This is what we call "forgetting."*

The girl was thirsty.

Her cheeks were hollow and her hair formed a knot on her neck, hair barely combed. A prehistoric voice came out: "Did you have water on this boat?"

They were hoarse, drawled words, for a question that carried in itself an obsessive refrain. It wasn't a question in the past, it invaded the present and lodged itself in the future: water, water, water, the girl's parched throat blazed up, multiplying in the throats of all. Nicola thought that food you could get, although it was difficult, but water was different and without it no one would survive.

"So is there water on your boat or not?"

Her white shoes were new and inadequate. The tips were covered with mud: a dark winter had been laid on that unseasonable summer.

"We can go together to look for some," the child answered, pointing to the city. He had just set foot on the ground and hadn't much desire to return to the boat.

"If there was any do you think I would have asked you?"

The crowd pushed forward and the sailors began to disembark. It was an instant, and against the flow, through an invisible opening, the girl managed to slip onto the boat. Water, thought Nicola, means many things: the salt water of the sea that had buried the world, the stagnant water of the cellar in Piazza San Filippo that had been useful for survival, the water like something dazzling that drove the girl to get on an unknown boat.

The sailor who had taken the silverware was not among the soldiers arriving on land. Probably he had lingered inside and wouldn't be pleased to find an intruder. Nicola decided to turn back.

At first he saw no one. His relief increased when he saw her, slaking her thirst from the barrels on board. Water, water, water.

A cold shadow rested on the boy's shoulder. Here he was, the man to whom he had handed over the silver in exchange for safety.

"I was good to you and you repay me by letting your aunt sneak on?"

The girl was frightened. The water she'd been gulping had ended up on her cloak and her hair, mussing it and curling it even more, while her deep, frightened eyes sought a way to flee.

"Is that how they teach you to behave? Like a thief?"

The soldier advanced.

"Maybe in your parts that's the custom. As for us, they teach us to risk our life to save others. I will die under one of your buildings or burned by one of your fires, and I will have died for a population of thieves."

He stopped. "Because it's clear that the Lord has punished you. He wouldn't have struck down a people if that people hadn't deserved it."

The girl gained a space between the sailor's body and the door, breathed in to get into her lungs as much air as possible, and took a run-up; but the man immobilized her, folding her arms behind her back.

"I brought you your nephew, I ferried him safe and sound, and you didn't even say thank you."

The girl looked at Nicola, uncomprehending.

"Thank you," she entreated, trying to get free, but the soldier pushed one hand against her breast and squeezed it, then stuck the other under her skirt. His broad back covered her entire body, starting something for which there were no words. Fight, clash, battle are words that imply a confrontation between equals, and yet there was no equality in what happened. The girl tried to scream, the sailor took off his cap and used it to stop up her mouth, pushed her to the floor and began to move on top of her.

Three torpedoes and four cannons. During the crossing Nicola had reflected that the weapons on the small, heavy torpedo boat *Morgana* could kill them all, the people of Messina, those of Reggia. That thought helped him keep at bay a worse thought, about the most disturbing and dangerous weapon on board: that sailor's gaze. The eyes most like his mother's he'd ever seen.

"You stood there staring to learn how it's done?" the soldier said to him with a sneer, as he left. Nicola remained petrified, incapable of responding. His voice was hidden in the depths of his throat, disappeared, vanished.

The girl had stood up, and had a vacant expression. She no longer seemed of this Earth. Her hair was crushed against her neck. She passed by him, and she, too, left, without saying a word.

# THE FEMALE POPE

*Here is a* woman, *she is* seated; *she wears a* three-layered tiara; *a* veil *is suspended above her head to cover the intermediate planes that she does not want to perceive; and she is looking at an* open book *on her knees.*

I fled the torpedo boat *Morgana* wondering if there existed a place on earth where I could hide forever. Of all the splinters that were still falling on my city, I had not avoided the sharpest. It had pierced me at a point near the heart and I would not be able to clean its ineradicable filth.

I had never boarded a ship before, even though I had gazed endlessly at the ferries, dreaming of embarking and escaping far away. Instead, when I set foot on one, I had been pushed back, down, lower than I had believed possible, and it was my own fault, my arrogance, the conviction that I could make it myself.

Compared with what I was living, the crash that two nights before had hurled me from the window into the street seemed a gentle breath. Then I was gravely damaged, now I was ruined irremediably.

Annihilated and limping, I looked for a street that would lead me home.

Yes, but what home? What place would I call home now? Certainly I couldn't return to my father's house, assuming it remained standing and assuming he was numbered among the survivors: impure and broken, I would be definitively useless. Marriage to the man whose surname I didn't want to utter—again, if he was alive—with the loss of my purity fell off his horizon, and if I was not a dowry what could I be? Nothing good, nothing other than trouble. No, I would not have wanted to encounter my father. The news that arrived about the individual towns along the coast was sketchy and contradictory, and, besides, I had no nostalgia for Scaletta Zanclea and its ill-hung doors, among which I hadn't been happy. Without my father, the giddy excitement of considering myself alone had urged me to walk free and bold in the city where I had lost everything but my body, and until I boarded the *Morgana* I thought that that body was my good fortune, because the earthquake had spared it and the sea hadn't killed it. I was wrong.

My wholeness was a deception, the disguise of a greater abuse. I wasn't invincible and that body wasn't mine, in fact he who had wanted it had taken it—he who could, as soon as he could. The earthquake had been a general proof of my destruction, but the earth is never satisfied; it can't be. Until that moment I had believed that my destiny would be sad but not impossible to face, I had saved myself from death to be present at the death of others, to be surprised by the horror of corpses dragged by streams along with the foundations of buildings, to endure the torture of knowing where my grandmother was buried without being able to dig her out. Becoming invisible had been a painful and feverish shock; it incited in me an unknown consciousness, of having survived to bear witness, perhaps even to write about what had happened. A high task, a noble fate, until, punctually, the punishment had arrived: I wasn't dead because I would have a slow and agonizing end.

I went to the Riviera Ringo and across from the Church of Gesù e Maria del Buonviaggio found a corner of beach where I could wash. I began by scrubbing the clothes until the cloak was soaked and worn through, then I went on to clean myself forcefully under the skirt, too, on the bare skin. Finally, no longer distinguishing between the water of my tears and the water of the Strait, without even taking off my shoes, I went into the sea wishing not to emerge.

The statues of the Madonna and her son, behind me on the façade of the religious building, held oil lamps offering light for sailors leaving to go fishing, for journeys and returns. The church had survived the earthquake, and the sculptures with it. The care that God had for men always survived, I noted with hatred, and even that woman and holy mother had protected not me but them. I wept with rage and filth, I stuck my head under the water and tried to fill my lungs with liquid, hoping the current would carry me out to sea. If my sea had become a cemetery, I wanted to be one of its corpses, a body in an aquarium of bodies, a fossil in an ossuary. I stopped thinking.

Soon afterward, my back bumped against a sandy shore, and I opened my eyes more in anger than in surprise. I hadn't left the coast. I remained unbearably alive: the sea hadn't wanted me, I was no good even at killing myself.

A hand grabbed my face, another my hair. Jutta dragged me onto the shore, calling me by name.

She undressed me and dried me with a blanket, I was naked in front of her, she would see that I was no longer a virgin and intact.

I was naked before anyone, ruined without possibility of repair. I yelled at her to leave me in peace, I wanted to die and no one would prevent me, but she dragged me farther up until the shore stopped licking my feet and the strength to oppose her failed.

It began to drizzle. A light yellowish water grimed our skin, our clothes. Jutta asked me to go with her to the church, where we would be sheltered safely.

"Someone bothered you, right?" she asked, staring at me. I shook my head no, fiercely. No one should know, not even her. She didn't respond and threw me a pile of black material. It was a garment of strict mourning, of poor quality, used many times. If I couldn't die I would live with death on me. I wore the widowhood of a stranger and her worn-out sorrow was superimposed on my skin.

The Ringo church was full of sacks and pieces of material used as beds. We looked for a corner for ourselves, but there were already too many people and the floor was so crowded you could barely walk, so I proposed to Jutta that we go back together to the nuns of Santa Teresa who had housed me the night before. I added that first she would have to go with me to a place, I had to look for someone. She agreed, and we set out. She was still visibly limping, and at her shins her clothes were thick with dark, by now old blood.

On the way I asked her how she had been able to find me. She had waited until she had had a terrible foreboding, a vision, as if a black door had been slammed shut before her, so she had started looking for me at the Marina and, not seeing me anywhere, had begun to stop strangers randomly, describing what I looked like. Few had paid attention to her, and those few had shaken their heads, but a woman, a woman alone, had said she knew me and yes, I had got off a torpedo boat and headed toward the Ringo.

The foreboding had grown; Jutta had been tortured by murky, diabolical images. Unfortunately, she said, because of the pain in her limbs she had been unable to go as quickly as she wished and had feared she wouldn't be in time to save me, even if she didn't know from what.

I grabbed her arm, squeezed it hard. No one, apart from her and the nuns, had been kind to me, no one had worried if I was dead or alive, if I had food and clothing, a place for the night. No one had wanted to share an indivisible solitude or let the egoism of survival be diminished by the possibility of doing it with someone else.

"Thank you," I said to Jutta, moved. The last time I had uttered those words I had done it to save myself, and it hadn't worked. Now on my lips there was intention and truth, and yet I was no longer sure it was enough. But beside me was Jutta, and that was already so much.

"For love of your grandmother, I can't leave you alone," she said.

We continued arm in arm in the rain, she wrapped in delicate green wool and I in thick worn black cotton. Dressed as a widow, I led her to the entrance of the cemetery, and then inside, discovering that it wasn't empty or untouched, as I'd hoped. Among the shattered graves and tombs buried by other tombs, not even the dead had been spared by death. I headed to the corner where I had dreamed so often of going, while around us people wept and prayed on the graves of their loved ones. I wasn't the only one who'd had the idea of seeking comfort from ghosts, but we were all alone, each with our own spectres. Jutta followed me in silence, occasionally pausing at a stone to utter a blessing. An image of Letteria Montoro was sticking out from the rubble of her ruined grave: I had no need to read the name to recognize the woman who had been so important for me, cancelled as the stories of women are always cancelled. I had lost her book, *Maria Landini*, but one day I would find it again and be reunited with those precious pages. I searched for some surviving words, sitting to rummage among the fragments of the epigraph: ". . . oblivion will not weigh on her ashes . . . ," ". . . she sacrificed her life in a Christian manner . . ." Here, finally: ". . . a woman of free spirit . . ." I hugged the precious phrase and put it in my pocket as if it were my due: the lost book was restored to me. The marble where those words were written was mine, and that was just. I kissed the photo, flaking but clear, and after a moment's hesitation I put that, too, in my pocket.

"A beautiful woman, your mother," Jutta said only then.

And I didn't deny it and answered yes, she was.

# THE FOOL

*[A] man walking, in the clothes of a buffoon, holding a bag and supporting himself with a staff, which he does not use to chase away the dog attacking him.*

The silence smelled of metal and terror. Holding his breath, his body crushed behind the barrels, Nicola didn't move a muscle. He had heard footsteps, after the girl left, and had been afraid that the sailor would return to do to him what he had done to her. If there was something he was good at, better than anyone, it was remaining motionless: he had done it every night of his life, with or without the ropes that tied him to the bed. Now the bed had become a vertical wall, the need not to exist in order to save his life had remained the same as ever, a torpedo boat had taken the place of the cellar, and Maria wasn't dead, she was embodied in the demon eyes of a sailor. Vincenzo, Maria: the male devil and the female devil in the tarot cards subjugated a third being, half male and half female—or was it he who controlled them? Vincenzo, Maria, the sailor. The sadistic trio of the card turned over by Madame was complete.

Voices of men laughing, soldiers shouting. Behind the barrels, the shadow of a hidden boy.

The torpedo boat *Morgana* raucously weighed anchor.

It's impossible, Nicola thought, and ran toward the exit, imagining diving in and swimming to land. He was afraid, he had never stopped being afraid. He had gone there to be safe, Messina was the only place he knew, apart from Reggio, and now he was leaving it again. Running, he heard footsteps, and, even more fearful of being discovered, he looked for another hiding place. In the dark he realized he was shaking. The barrels and the walls of the ship were shaking along with him, jolted by the engine. Where would he end up? He was afraid of finding himself in a strange city, with incomprehensible dialects and alien streets. In Messina he knew how to get to the cathedral, he knew the shops, and the accent of the inhabitants wasn't different from his and his father's. Had the devil boarded the ship? And if, seeing him, he killed him? If he did to him what he had just done to the girl from Messina?

Nicola breathed softly, tried to hold his breath beyond the limits. The voices came closer.

"I had to take on three of them!" one laughed.

"Without husbands they've gone mad . . ." said a second.

"They were just waiting for the earthquake to display their true nature."

"They're all like that here."

"My cousin had himself sent on purpose to Messina for the women—all *whoors*."

Among the soldiers' voices was also the devil's, no longer alone, but one among many. Together, as they had approached, they left. Nicola breathed again.

How long would the voyage last? Where were they headed?

To distract himself, the boy began to count.

Once he got to a million they would land in Naples, he said to himself. Five hundred and four, five, six. They landed. Where had they arrived in such a short time?

He kept counting, listening to the din diminish.

When he was sure he was alone, he gathered his courage and slipped outside. Again the dock, the port. The starry night, the calm sea, a destroyed and familiar landscape.

He had returned to Reggio Calabria.

# FORCE

*This is the Arcanum of Force. What, therefore, does the eleventh Arcanum of the Tarot teach? Through the very tableau that it represents, it says: the Virgin tames the lion and thereby invites us to leave the plane of quantity—for the Virgin is evidently weaker than the lion concerning the quantity of physical force—and to raise ourselves to the plane of quality, for it is evidently there that the superiority of the Virgin over the lion is to be found.*

For their farewell to 1908 in the devastated city, the sisters had prepared a dinner with what they could scrape together, bread and dried fish but also unknown sweets, from Sicilian cities where I had never been. They had received a makeshift kitchen, but it would not be functional until the new year, so in the meantime we made do by mixing food that was already cooked. They told us that in Catania and Palermo grand carts filed by, collecting donations for the poor evacuees of Messina. The donors were exaggeratedly generous in wishing for themselves a clean conscience and for us a less miserable palate.

That night we ate rice crepes and *cucuzzata*, a sweet jam made with long green squash. I tasted a spoonful, but it had gone bad: someone had put in some leftovers, taking advantage of the charity convoys to empty the pantry. The gelatin burned my tongue, the saliva reacted, producing a taste so acidic that I had to spit it all out. My stomach cramped, and I preferred to be alone; the nuns were used to the furtive melancholy that often drove me into a corner, and wouldn't try to intrude on a silence that was comfortable for me and off-putting to others. They wouldn't judge me. They had asked about my family, I had said they were all dead, and they hadn't questioned me further. They had welcomed Jutta and me as sisters in the shelters set up like a replica of the convent, and even if I didn't join the prayers they didn't exclude me from the services. Ever since I'd left the torpedo boat *Morgana*, god had lost the capital letter.

In the morning I waited for the nuns to finish washing so that I could spend a long time at it without pressure to give someone my place. Because the layers of filth were so thick that the normal amount of time wasn't enough. While I scrubbed my arms and legs I let myself cry, releasing the pent-up tears; then I felt observed by a child's eyes, eyes I didn't recognize: they stared at me unmoving, with their long black lashes, and slowly soothed me. My tears were used up, and, emptied, I could return to the sisters.

In those days, King Vittorio Emanuele III and Queen Elena were in the city, having sailed from Naples as soon as they learned of our disaster. They had descended from the royal ship amid applause and whistles from the Messinese, and the mayor had been at the forefront to welcome them.

"At least he reproached the sovereign for the fact that help arrived from abroad long before it came from the Italians," commented Mother Fortunata, the superior, defending the mayor. Rosalba had a different idea: "In fact it was the king who reminded him that he had fled for almost two days, abandoning us to our fate."

I admired Rosalba's ability always to say what she thought, and yet I couldn't be on her side, either. In neither version did I feel the truth, only the need to sanctify one man in order to sully another. The protagonists of that scene were two men, in uniform and protected by an institutional responsibility, just like the sailor from the *Morgana*: who was right and who was wrong didn't interest me. Who had played the part of the hero and who the enemy was a secondary detail, and reversible.

"Best is the queen, who boarded the *Campania*, where they set up a hospital for the youngest children," Sister Velia concluded, pragmatic, and they all agreed.

I, thinking of the scene of a woman who by herself captured a ship of men, couldn't say a word.

At night I began staring at a pile of toys. Donations arrived continuously for the children who had survived the earthquake, and many of them came through the sisters, who distributed them. I was hypnotized by those toys. A doll with hair of an artificial blond frightened me, and I was saddened by a toy version of the locomotive of the last train I had taken in my old life, on the night of December 27th, when I had stubbornly left Scaletta to go to the theater in Messina. Those objects recounted a world forbidden to me. I had grown up among adults who treated me like an equal, and I didn't remember playing with my contemporaries; as a child I read or studied, or learned to take care of the house, because that's what my father wanted. Childhood for me was a distant and imprecise place, and yet in the past two days a detail insisted on emerging, eyes with long lashes appeared by surprise, and interrogated me in a nervous and agitated darkness. Were they watching over me or abandoning me, I couldn't tell, I couldn't distinguish between the two verbs. Was it a memory? A dream? The manifestation of that gaze was painful, and I didn't want to sustain it, but the effort of erasing it wore me out, and I struggled to keep my eyes open. Sleep came long before a midnight when I had nothing to celebrate anyway.

The sovereigns were still in the city, and for the whole day we talked about Elena of Montenegro, glorified everywhere as the best queen in the history of Italy. Behind a language of false respect I noticed the sisters' disapproval: Elena had given gold watches to the military men who guided and protected her during the rescues, and was so distressed by the fate of the orphans that she had decided to establish an entire institution devoted to them. The silent reproach was that she hadn't deigned to go and see the nuns, to know from their living voices how many and what losses they'd had, what concrete help they were already giving the city. Between the waste of the jewelry, the echo of morbid compassion, and the halo of stubborn pride, the queen fell out of my heart. But the truth was different: it grieved me to think that the sailor from the *Morgana* might be among those rewarded.

I tossed and turned on the pile of clothes that served me as a bed, in the same room where the nuns ate, and I gave a sigh that must have resembled a lament. Jutta left the table and came to caress my hair. Her clothes gave off a citrus scent: the woman they'd belonged to must have been a fan of Fera bergamot, and its traces on her clothes remained recognizable for a long time. My mother had also used it, long before it became famous in the rest of Italy.

"You smell like the woods," I said.

"You're a hunting dog," she laughed, and sniffed her arms in search of confirmation. "When I put on clothes that aren't mine I always think of who's looking for them and can no longer find them," she continued, bringing a hem of the skirt to her nose. "The dead observe us. But I'm more afraid that the living will come looking for us."

"The living are all dead."

"Today I heard the story of a wife and husband who were reunited. Each thought the other was dead."

"There are all kinds of stories like that."

"You wouldn't like to hug your father again?"

"If I could choose, I would feel my mother's skin. I hardly remember her anymore."

Jutta caressed my hair again, as she did whenever she felt I was in the grip of uncontrollable thoughts, and she stayed with me so that I wouldn't be alone. The voices faded, and a last silvery sound remained of dishes cleared.

My sleep was agitated. The sailor's body was above me, it became a fish and then a goat, it held me firm and stared at me. The animals entered my uterus and spread it to bursting. I woke sweaty and screaming, and I couldn't get up because the room was spinning; along with Jutta, Sister Rosalba came to calm me.

From then on, every night had its nightmares. My darkness was populated with bright-colored chinchillas and ringing voices, wild boars, deformed whales. Once a fly aimed at my stomach and smashed it, I was thrown against the bottom of the bed while hands of gigantic beings twisted my head from my neck. Sister Rosalba confessed to me that this had happened to her, too, before entering the convent, and so her parents had been happy to get rid of that unquiet and disquieting daughter who wouldn't let them sleep and frightened them. I had a great fear of being a burden to the sisters in difficult times, so I worked hard at keeping our encampment in order. I organized the food and washed and hung up the clothes, trying to be useful to the women, intent, in turn, on being useful to the world. I abandoned the streets until I forgot the city and annulled myself in the work; if in the nuns' gaze I read assent or approval I felt reassured, they wouldn't throw me out. Rosalba brought me the best present I could have wished for, a book, and one written by a woman. Someone had thrown in Matilde Serao's *Neapolitan Legends* among the provisions and clothes in a charity package; I hid it among my few intimate possessions, along with the two fragments from the tombstone of Letteria Montoro and a diamond that Jutta had taken from her finger and wanted me to have at all costs.

"If we should lose each other and you need help, sell it," she said.

"And if it were you who needed it?" I was distressed.

"I'll manage," she concluded.

For the sisters Jutta was invaluable. She served as an interpreter in the conversations with foreign soldiers and volunteers, translating from German, French, English. She was always outside, on the threshold, while I didn't want to see anyone, and stayed shut up in the encampment, where men's voices came to me muffled.

Every so often some women stopped by; I could tolerate speaking with them. One night Sister Rosalba introduced a Frenchwoman who wanted to meet the nuns of the monastery of Santa Teresa, now famous because they had not abandoned their places, more concerned with doing good for others than for themselves. She, too, was considered invaluable on both sides of the Strait, because she could sense the presence of the dead, and the soldiers brought her along to learn where to dig without wasting time. Thanks to Madame, said Sister Rosalba, many had been rescued still alive.

"Come, tell the story of Filippo," she urged, with the excitement of one who has already heard the astonishing story and is eager to enjoy the reactions of others.

Madame told of a child saved eight days after the disaster. The soldiers wanted to set off a mine to destroy the remains of a dangerous building, but first, out of some scruple, they sent for her, to be sure that no one was buried in the ruins. Madame interrogated the air and the splintered beams with all five senses, and then she stopped the operation: yes, someone was there. The soldiers started digging at the point she indicated. I thought I had observed that scene, directed not by a diviner but by a mother, and yet, in fact, it was incredible that here the person who sensed a presence knew nothing about that house and had no blood ties to nourish the persistence. My admiration for Madame rose, clothing itself in reverence and fear. The Frenchwoman recounted that, once the child emerged, he said he had endured so long thanks to oranges given by his mother's loving hands, and he wasn't afraid because her voice continued to cradle him. No one had had the heart to contradict him, but Filippo's mother had died three years earlier, as the inhabitants of Scaletta Zanclea had confirmed.

Hearing the name of my town I felt a pang.

"You were in Scaletta." I started. "Do you have news of Giuseppe Ruello?"

Madame stared at me. "The merchant? He's the one who took Filippo with him, he wants to adopt him. He said he'd always wanted a male heir, but his wife died shortly after giving him a girl. He came here to Messina to look for his daughter and his mother, but they're both dead. Why do you ask specifically about him?"

Fear, dismay, an uncontrollable desire to hide: the storm that crashed down on me at those words was violent and unexpected. And then why in the world had my father chosen that particular boy, what was special about him, why had he impressed him. I tried to conceal my feelings, struggling between the desire to see him again and the anguish of losing the freedom that solitude gave me, a freedom I'd never had.

"He was a distant cousin of my grandmother's," I lied.

I had the sensation that some of the sisters read the lie in my face, but Jutta changed the subject and I took advantage of that to recover.

Although Sister Rosalba insisted that Madame was a Christian, the woman wore no crucifixes, she didn't have the look of a saint, and she ignored things having to do with prayers, miracles, and divine intercessions. The older sisters were suspicious. Was she a witch? The number of the saved was undeniable, as was the gentleness of her manner and her usefulness, and yet if Madame had not taken out a good sum and given it into the hands of the superior, maybe she would not have been invited to spend the night. Only then, in fact, did Mother Fortunata set aside an ill-concealed distrust.

After we ate, we learned that among Madame's gifts was the reading of the tarot. Murmurs and laughter broke out: Christians were not permitted to predict the future. Mother Fortunata recalled the biblical episode of the Witch of Endor.

"Saul bans necromancers and diviners from the kingdom," she thundered.

"But he asks his ministers to find a palm reader, because the Lord doesn't respond," Sister Rosalba continued.

A discussion followed in which the Mother did not retract, but, when she took her leave, Sister Rosalba and others approached the clairvoyant, and Jutta followed them.

"Friends and sisters, I'm tired, and I have to conserve my energy for what there is still to do in these lands," Madame began, "but I want to repay you for welcoming me, and I can grant one card to a single one of you. If I did more I would be cheating you: I don't have sufficient strength."

She asked us not to cross arms or legs, and to stay at a distance of a meter. Then she pulled the deck out of a white leather glove she had in her pocket. In a silence saturated with curiosity, we observed Madame while she shuffled the cards. None of us dared breathe. It was she who chose.

"You." She raised her chin in my direction.

I didn't answer. My heart was beating madly. I thought I was finished: the foreign fortune teller wanted to unmask me, she had understood that I was the living daughter of that Ruello in Scaletta and she would take me back to my father, she would spread in the city the rumor that I wasn't dead at all. And that I was impure, broken. I wanted to escape, but she was faster, she cut the deck and showed me the card, naming it without need of verifying it.

"To the Empress."

A blonde in the blue robe of a ruler, adorned with gold jewelry, wearing a crown, and sitting on a throne, stared at me with a compassionate expression. Her gaze was directed at me and, at the same time, elsewhere, as if the scepter that with her left hand she planted on her stomach were a magic door, contact with a universe familiar to her but invisible to us. Because of the ambiguous folds, the fabric behind her could be confused with a pair of wings, but her feet rested solid on the ground: the Empress belonged the sky and the earth. A lion was pictured on the shield clutched in her right hand. I was amazed to realize that the beast didn't frighten me.

Jutta was the first to speak. "What does it mean?"

"You'll be a mother," Madame responded, not to her but to me.

# THE POPE

*Now, benediction is more than a simple good wish
made for others; it is also more than a magical
impress of personal thought and will upon others.
It is the putting into action of divine power,
transcending the individual thought and will of
the one who is blessed as well as the one who is
pronouncing the blessing. In other words it is an
essentially* sacerdotal *act.*

When you don't know where to go, you always go home. If the house
isn't there, you go anyway. Even on the mangled, twisted streets of a
snarling night, Nicola, fleeing the port, would have found the way
from the Marina to Piazza San Filippo with his eyes closed; he climbed
over ruins that had once been buildings, inventing new shortcuts; he
went faster when he had to escape and hid at every perceived danger.
The darkness was sweet, dense with insects and rustling sounds, and
the child soon learned to distinguish them. If you trusted it, night in
the city without borders might resemble a bed.

Reaching the square, he stopped. The last contours of the house
could barely be distinguished. The cellar, however, was still in its place.

Nicola raised the trapdoor. He could sleep outside, on the grass, or go inside, as instinct suggested. And if a stranger surprised him, an undesired guest? In Reggio the houses belonged to everyone, each person chose for himself where to sleep, where to live. But who would dare to appropriate a cellar crowded with presences?

If another human being had tried to usurp his bed, the demons would give him no peace. He alone could speak to them, he who had known them forever. And if the sailor looked for him there, the monsters and cats of the night would protect him. Yes, he was sure of it: the ghosts were his family, no earthquake had murdered them.

Without hesitating any longer he went down the stairs and, reaching the bottom, looked for the bier so he could curl up on it. He was no longer alone as before: now Maria and Vincenzo were sleeping not above his head but dug in near him, somewhere in the shelter of the walls. Father, mother, who are now in my cellar: rest, I forgive you, he prayed in his mind, falling into a sleep without nightmares.

The next morning, a series of dull, similar days began. With the light, Nicola went out and got food and water. Food was within reach: you had only to enter the most sumptuous houses, and he was well aware of which they were; he knew the surnames of the wealthy, their addresses, knew their windows and doors. Inside, it was easy to guess the kitchens and fill his pockets. He never went twice to the same place, he left no traces and stole only food, no lamps, no silverware or objects of value. The first house he stole from was Dalila's, his mother's friend who had almost had him killed; from her closet he took a bag and put in it cans that then he didn't touch: the provisions of that poisonous woman might also be poison, so better to pack them under the bier for an emergency.

With the darkness, Nicola returned to the cellar. The second night he pulled a chest up the stairs and from then on, before going to sleep, he blocked the entrance to lock himself in. They slept soundly, he and the ghosts. Maria and Vincenzo, wherever they might be, were finally silent.

Only two people appeared to him at night: the girl and the sailor. Of her Nicola saw again the slender legs under his body, the glassy gaze when she passed by him, as if the soldier, mounting her, had consumed her soul. Of him he heard his contemptuous, sarcastic voice, what he had said to him: Look, learn how it's done. Then he woke up and swore that one day, when he was grown, he would track down that man and kill him, so he would no longer be able to harm anyone. That thought devoured him, sleep fled, and a heavy exhaustion enveloped him. He picked up his magazines to read over and over again the adventures of his beloved *Cadetti di Guascogna*.

Gradually the streets of Reggio Calabria grew crowded with children begging for care and charity. One afternoon, carrying Dalila's bag overflowing with stolen provisions, he heard himself called loudly by name. In two of the beggars he recognized some schoolmates, sisters, one younger than him and one older. He lowered his cap and ran away. The next morning he was more careful not to be recognized by anyone: he pulled up his jacket collar and settled the hat almost over his eyes. In reality he had plenty of food, but leaving the cellar for several hours was his only contact with the air, a way to reassure himself that the city was still in its place, devastated but real. There was a gloomy yellow rain, the muddy air became hard to breathe, and Nicola decided to go home. Returning to the ruins of his old house he found a surprise.

The younger of the sisters who had called to him the day before was sitting near the trapdoor, under a plane tree. She was wearing a gray dress held up with some pins, certainly not a child's dress.

"Nicola, don't you remember? I'm Emma Battista."

Nicola didn't answer.

"Don Franco told us to look for children who've been left without their mamma and papa. Yours are dead, right?"

Nicola signaled no and looked around in search of a way to flee. What did they want from him?

"Don Franco gives us food and we sleep in the church all together. A priest is arriving soon, sent by the Pope, and he'll take us to a shelter. You mustn't be afraid."

Nicola didn't want to go anywhere, he wanted to stay in the cellar.

"They'll arrest the children who don't come."

While his schoolmate was talking, Nicola saw her face disintegrate, to be replaced by the face of before. The emaciated, livid Emma, with dirty hair, who was gesturing inside the clothes of a grandmother, gave way to a girl the same age as him, properly dressed, plump, with clear skin and a serene expression.

"You mustn't be ashamed. My parents are dead, too, and also my brother. Camilla and I are left."

Nicola was surprised, he didn't remember a boy coming out of school with them.

"He had the same name as you. He was two months old." Emma lowered her head, holding back her tears.

It hadn't stopped raining. The embroidery on her dress had stuck to her small chest, where the material bunched up. An owl, a dove, or a bat wheeled above their heads. Nicola couldn't tell what sort of creature it was because, although he tried to concentrate on the beating wings, he couldn't raise his eyes from the ground. He wanted to cry, too, he wanted to hug Emma, to shout that none of what had happened was right, but his strength abandoned him, his legs gave way. He squatted on the grass hugging his knees, and curled up hoping that the earth would swallow them both.

"Why don't you speak?" Emma asked, pulling on his sleeve.

At that moment Nicola realized that he hadn't talked to anyone since the girl left the torpedo boat. And even before, while the man attacked her, he had said nothing. He tried to answer Emma. His voice wouldn't emerge.

He huddled into himself even more vigorously.

"Let's go," she urged him sweetly again and again, while Nicola kicked and the rain lessened.

Was he really sure he wanted to remain alone, shut in the cellar, forever? He felt something in his heart yield and give way. Emma was so little, so full of trust even in the future. He couldn't leave her alone, or something terrible would happen to her, as it had to the girl on the *Morgana*.

"Let's go," she repeated, and in the end he followed her.

Nicola spent only a few nights in Don Franco's parish church. Emma brought three other children besides him, Camilla seven; others had just arrived or had been camping there for several weeks. In all they were twenty-two. Twenty-two orphans of the earthquake, whose fate the Pope was deciding, so said the priest. Pius X is always thinking of you, he repeated, and don't listen to those who tell you the contrary! The Pope prays unceasingly: you are not without a father, he is your father on Earth, as God is in Heaven, pray, pray.

The canned meat was hard and salty, but in midafternoon there were always hot donuts made by a woman who lived nearby, and there was never any shortage of water. In the days before, Nicola had learned to drink from puddles and functioning fountains, but only now did he really satisfy his thirst; his throat became cool and even his sight cleared, as if it had been clouded by dryness. The first night in the church he couldn't sleep: he had never slept with others. The second night, Emma settled beside him and under the covers entwined her legs around his. The child stank of sweat and her breath was sour, but her body was warm and reassuring.

"I love you," she said, and Nicola believed her, because, even if they had never spoken before the earthquake, it was what he, too, had felt, ever since they met face to face in front of the trapdoor.

Unfortunately he couldn't say it. He hadn't opened his mouth since he disembarked from the torpedo boat.

"Don't worry, Nicolino. Another mamma and another papa will do for us: ours have become angels."

Two devils, he thought, couldn't become angels.

"Reggio no longer exists," Emma said again, repeating the words of the adults. Nicola didn't want to hear it. Reggio existed, damaged but alive, destroyed but still the same. Where there were houses there would be caverns, where there were streets they could make paths: it would be simple to survive. Twenty-two children together were an entire people, if they had all wanted it, if they had been left to do it. And yet, apart from Nicola, it seemed that no one could wait to have a new papa and a new mamma.

# THE EMPRESS

*The third Arcanum of the Tarot, being the arcanum
of sacred magic, is by this very fact, the arcanum of
generation. For generation is only an aspect of the
sacred magic. If sacred magic is the union of two
wills—human and divine—from which a miracle
results, generation itself also presupposes the trinity
of the generator, the generant and the generated.*

The night Madame drew the Empress card for me I was visited
not by nightmares but by a complete and transparent dream,
studded with marvelous details. I was in a meadow without large
buildings or houses, my eyes were lost in a green expanse, and a
childish voice was calling me mamma. When it was silent, Jutta
intervened, asking: So, isn't it nice to be called that? Although I
couldn't see her, I felt that my friend was beside me, and her kind
presence eased my astonishment. In fact it's not bad, I replied, but
I would like to know who it is, and whether male or female? Jutta
asked me to turn, and in the middle of the meadow, behind me, a
very tall stalk ended in a white flower, halfway between a camellia
and an orchid. Its was the voice: I had a flower child.

I woke disturbed, and convinced myself that, if Madame's words were true, to become a mother in the future wouldn't be frightening. In recent days I had surprised myself thinking that to live beside a man didn't necessarily have to be a torture, and the thought always returned to Vittorio Trimarchi. I had had no news of him, but I knew that Professor Gaetano Salvemini had remained buried under the ruins of the house he rented in Messina, along with his wife, his sister, and five children. And Vittorio? Since discovering that my father was alive I'd made no assumptions and stopped believing in presentiments; I resigned myself to waiting for the results of collisions and encounters with reality.

Sometime later, while I was organizing the donations, my breathing slowed down and then it stopped altogether. I couldn't breathe, the air around me hid, fled. The lack of air forced me to sit down; gasping, I managed to call Rosalba, who in turn hurried to tell Jutta. My friends decided to give me a sedative, afraid I was no longer myself, but I didn't want anything, my body was closed, armored, I shouted to protect myself, they mustn't try to give me anything. I calmed down only out of fear that someone would hear me and take me away. The lunatics of the earthquake, as those who weren't willing to be silent and submissive were called, were shut up in the Villa di Salute, the hospital for the mentally ill established by Dr. Lorenzo Mandalari. The doctor had died on the night of December 28th, but the structure had remained standing; it was said that many patients escaped, taking advantage of the confusion, while new guests had been interned against their will. Every time I was about to give in to anxiety and anger, I was afraid of being reported and taken there, so I held back tears and cries, suffocated my anger and swallowed the excess; that time, too, I pushed everything back inside, fear above all.

My shortness of breath didn't go away. I was no longer efficient at organizing our camp; every so often lungs, heart, stomach rose into my throat begging me to spit them out, and I started panting again, moving to a corner so as not to be seen. While I cleaned I wasn't able to speak, if Jutta asked me a question I had to stop and catch my breath. I blamed the negative feelings I lived with. The memory of the violence on the *Morgana* clung to me like a malignant vine. The earthquake no, I was used to it, we had all become used to it.

As soon as I woke I smelled bad odors from the kitchen, and for the entire day food disgusted me. The sisters put meat and fish on the table, the shopkeepers resumed their activities, huts rose on Viale San Martino that sold even imported foodstuffs: tripe, sturgeon, Gruyère, eggs. And meanwhile the soldiers continued to distribute the daily ration for the homeless, a hundred and fifty grams of pasta and, very occasionally, half a can of meat. The pantries filled up again, but I wasn't hungry.

One morning Sister Velia, who had the best instinct for shopping, boasted of having acquired the finest cuts of meat, and at lunch prepared a great mixed platter: boiled beef, liver, prized fillet. The odor of the dried blood of dead creatures passed through clothes and stuck to the skin; I made an effort to repress my nausea, but when Rosalba filled my plate I had to run away and throw up.

"Does she know, our Barbara, that she's spitting out food worth three lire a kilo?" Mother Fortunata was annoyed. "You know how many starving people would like to be in her place?"

Jutta came to me with a rag soaked in vinegar, she laid it on my forehead and the smell calmed me.

"You're pregnant," she said. "I've been watching, since the day of the torpedo boat, and I hoped to be wrong, but now we have to make a decision."

So much noise in my ears, a cannon shot.

"How can you be sure? You don't have children, you don't know anything about pregnancy."

"A few years ago I gave birth to a stillborn child. For nine months I held it in my belly, I know what it's like, I look at you and see myself again. Don't worry. It will go differently for you, your child will live if you want it."

No, no, no. My head said: It's not true. My body said: Yes, it is.

I saw my end and an oppressive weeping assailed me. Everyone would know what I had done with the sailor, the sisters wouldn't believe me, they wouldn't believe that I hadn't wanted it, and maybe they were right, I hadn't opposed him forcefully enough, I had provoked him, I had boarded the ship alone. I was afraid of being killed, I had been complicit—why, why had I not preferred to die? I wasn't a saint, I was a coward, a worthless woman.

As long as there was no proof, I had deluded myself that in the future I would be able to live as if it hadn't happened: Messina would rise again, and I, too, with it. In the wounds of the city I would hide my own. Then I would forget that man and the torpedo boat, there would remain only the nightmare of a girl devastated by a disaster.

Of course, a husband would have to accept me already used, but to a man like Vittorio I would open my heart, I would be liberated, and together we would abolish that terrible dream, maybe we wouldn't have children or maybe we would; I would be free to go to the university, that promised desk had been waiting for me since December 27th, a desk of my own, where I could study and better myself. A rich drapery would be placed over my shoulders, like the Empress's, and finally I would be master of my world.

You will be a mother, Madame had predicted. My belly was already full and I didn't know it, no one knew it except the stranger who in a single encounter had brought me three items of news: my father was alive, I had an adopted brother, and an invisible creature was growing inside me.

Jutta repeated that I mustn't worry, we would manage. I begged her to find one of those women who would help me go back to the way I was before. I was willing to leave just to hurry the abortion, I had heard talk of a tisane of parsley and douching with soap, my grandmother had told me what imprudent girls had to endure, and the risk didn't matter to me, dying didn't matter to me, I wouldn't make the same mistake of cowardice again. Anyway, with that sin, what life would I have?

Jutta let me vent. Then, delicately, she spoke: "Barbara," she said. "Barbara, Barbara." My name on her lips was a cradle rocking, a sedative. "Barbara," she repeated again, and then, in her sharp accent and her perfect Italian: "It's not the existence we had before, it's another time. There's no hope here, at most there are miracles. We have death around us and you have life inside."

I didn't know if Jutta convinced me, with her eyes like water in mine so earthly, or if her words, with the emphasis on "life," simply encouraged the madness of paying attention to the creature nested inside me. Whatever its origin, from that moment it was no longer possible for me to ignore its presence. I began to imagine it.

It pushed its feet against my belly until I vomited, and slept on my diaphragm, making me sob or stopping my breath.

It came to me on the last day of 1908 and would be the first of all the New Years; it was the edge of the inferno and the leap into the void, the most mistaken choice and the only just destiny.

# THE HERMIT

*The Hermit is neither deep in meditation or study nor is he engaged in work or action. He is walking. This means to say that he manifests a third state beyond that of contemplation and action. He represents— in relation to the binary "knowledge—will" or "contemplation—action" or, lastly, "head—limbs"— the term of synthesis, namely that of heart. For it is the heart where contemplation and action are united, where knowledge becomes will and where will becomes knowledge. The heart does not need to forget all contemplation in order to act, and does not need to suppress all action in order to contemplate. It is the heart which is simultaneously active and contemplative, untiringly and unceasingly. It walks. It walks day and night, and we listen day and night to the steps of its incessant walking.*

Next to the chair where Sabina was sitting to drink her anti-influenza liqueur—with it, she always had a chocolate in the form of a flower, rose or camellia—was an old straw basket draped with blue material.

Issues of a magazine that was not in Nicola's old house were piled up in it: *La Donna* (*Woman*). It didn't resemble any of the newspapers Vincenzo bought; it seemed, rather, a version for ladies of the *Giornalino della Domenica*. Sabina, leafing through it, was very amused.

Nicola stood in the doorway of the big living room observing her. She had pale smooth skin, very black eyes, and an enormous bosom buttoned into a burgundy-colored silk shirt. She dangled her feet, rubbed her shoes with the buckle against each other, letting them fall to the floor, took a second chocolate, looked up and found Nicola staring at her. She smiled at him and it was as if the whole world were smiling.

"What are you doing there alone, come here," she urged him, huddling to one side of the green velvet chair to make room for him.

Nicola didn't move.

"Come to Mamma. You want to read me something? I know you can read: I saw you looking through the magazines."

For three days the Crestani husband and wife had tried in vain to make that mute child speak.

When Don Franco ordered his twenty-two orphans to dress as well as they could to meet with Monsignor Emilio Cottafavi, the papal envoy sent to Reggio Calabria to carry out the will of Pius X, Nicola had looked at Emma with a questioning expression, and she, as always, had intuited what the question was: Was that really him, the Pope's man?

"I remembered that his name was Don Orione, but this must be someone more important," she said, more confused than knowing. "That other one was supposed to take us to his shelter in Cassano allo Ionico, I don't know where this one's taking us," she added.

They had gone to the meeting, and there they'd found orphans from various parishes of the city and the area from Palmi to Gioia

Tauro. Nicola had never seen so many children all together; when Vincenzo and Maria were alive they had enrolled him in an exclusive private school in which boys and girls occupied two separate wings and caught glimpses of one another only on the way out, after the sound of the bell. Here, instead, in the big square where they gathered, boys sat next to girls, ages and sexes mixed in a great tumult, some covered their heads with caps fashioned by stretching a newborn's bonnet, some pulled over their knees a coat two sizes too small, some hid bruises and injuries on their knuckles or cheekbones, some clutched the hand of a sister or a friend, some acted tough, speaking in overly loud voices to make a show of not being scared. Nicola was very scared. He wondered if leaving his cellar had been the right choice; was he still in time to escape and live like a pirate or a thief? Who was now sleeping on his bier? Had the monsters stayed underground or vanished with the smoke of the fires after the earthquake? Had anyone recovered the bodies of Vincenzo and Maria, whom he continued to imagine as horned devils, even now that they were dead and buried?

Emma's small hand clutched his elbow. She had placed herself between him and Camilla, halfway between a guardian angel and a bodyguard. Believe me, said her posture, there's no reason to be afraid. Where did she find such courage and such trust.

When the Monsignor's hoarse voice rose, the children were suddenly silent. He was a corpulent man with a frowning expression, and he blinked his eyelids behind the glasses, as if he couldn't see well.

"The directives of our dearly beloved pontiff are clear," he began, and then: "Our Church is large, it will take care of you: the Calabrian children should stay in Calabria, the Sicilians in Sicily, and each of you has the right to receive a Catholic education. Nevertheless," he added, "in the days of the recovery many families in Italy have expressed a desire to help the orphans of these lands, and we believe that for you the right thing is to be welcomed into the warmth of a home: Who of us doesn't want to find again the warmth of the embrace we've lost? Who of us doesn't desire a mother and a father? To many loving couples the Lord has not given children. His will is inscrutable, yet today we understand the reasons: Their fate was not to bring forth new children of God but to adopt children already born. For those who have faith and patience," he concluded, "the moment always arrives when the mystery of our suffering becomes clear: You innocents are here to fulfill the will of God. The Lord has chosen you to make some suffering adults happy—are you ready for this task? The Lord summons you."

At those words Emma lit up, Camilla remained impassive, and Nicola grew pale.

The Monsignor listed the cities that had made themselves available to welcome the orphans; they were many, many were far away, and some Nicola had never heard of.

". . . and the very generous city of Biella, which will be able to take care of two hundred orphans."

Biella, strange name for a city, with an extra vowel that ruined a known adjective, *bella*, beautiful, what was Biella like, was it *bella*? With a convulsive laugh, Nicola turned to look at Emma and Camilla. Camilla smoothed the wrinkles of her dress over her knees. Nicola tugged Emma, who made him a sign to be quiet.

Soon afterward, every child was assigned a destination. Emma and Camilla's was Naples. But Nicola would go to Biella.

They spent the night in the same bed, all three of them. Emma's breath was no longer sour and Camilla's hair smelled of milk. The girls snored softly, Nicola didn't close his eyes.

The next day—with a bundle prepared by Don Franco that contained a change of underwear, a package of cookies, two rations of meat, and three bottles of water—Nicola wondered if it had been he himself who, with the power of his brain, had named that particular destination. Of the years with Maria, the years of nights tied to the bed and devils who threatened to seize him, the certainty had remained that it was he who controlled things: thoughts weren't only thoughts, the mind manipulated and originated the facts, sometimes blocked them. Shooting stars, the death of his parents, stopped clocks, and earthquakes were his fault. At the word Biella he had laughed, so God had decided to send him there.

"Bye, Nicolino, write to me," Emma said goodbye when the train stopped in Naples. "I'll get your address from Don Franco, I think once you're there you'll speak again." She was nearly crying as she shook him, and he couldn't respond, couldn't even open his mouth; he looked at her stupidly, as if all eleven years he had spent on the Earth had crashed down on him. Emma hurried to get off, dragging Camilla, before the train started again. She was the younger but acted as if she were the older: she would manage in Naples, she would manage anywhere. As for Nicola, he continued the journey.

"Come to Mamma," Sabina repeated, indulgently, putting down the magazine.

The child kept staring at her.

The mayor, a photographer, and a reporter had been waiting for him in Biella. He had had to pose, so that the city's daily paper could glorify the story of the arrival of the orphans of the earth-quake. Then they had gone to the town hall, and in a room of officials their names had been joined to other names.

"Fera, Nicola . . ." the official looked up from the register, "you go to the Crestanis!"

So a guard had led him on foot to a small pink building with wood-framed windows, surrounded by plane trees.

"Come and read something to Mamma."

Sabina's request became a plea. They had told her the child didn't speak because of the trauma: he wasn't born that way, they would have to be patient, give him time. Sabina was sure of it, but occasionally she had a suspicion that she wasn't enough, she wasn't a good mother, who knew what Nicola's mother had been like, the real one. A suffering expression escaped her, and he, noticing it, was sorry. Didn't the woman's patience, her sweetness deserve a reward? For three days Nicola had hidden. The first night he had slept under the bed, the second in the closet; he didn't answer if they called him, he ran away if they tried to caress him. He had eaten everything they put on the table, from pastina to wild game, he had scraped the plate with his fingers and licked them, although he knew it wasn't a polite gesture. He wanted to see if those two who had been introduced as his new mamma and his new papa would really love him. His heart said yes, fear said no, no, no. His head said: Now they'll send me away, now they'll send me away.

Nicola continued to watch them.

Giuseppe had thick gray hair and the same glasses frame as Monsignor Cottafavi. Unlike the monsignor, however, he often took off his glasses and he never blinked; in fact he kept his eyes open. Sabina seemed more like a daughter than a wife; with a cheerful, ringing voice she had run toward him on the street, but Nicola had retreated. Sabina smelled of fresh flowers, she changed her blouse two or three times a day, all the blouses were silk and made in Switzerland: Nicola knew that because he had glimpsed the labels and addresses of the shops on the boxes when she took them out.

The sideboard in the living room was laden with sweets to celebrate his arrival. He had taken the candies he liked best, with carob, and put them in his pocket, without saying a word. Sabina and Giuseppe had looked at each other, worried, but had let him do it. Who knows what he had seen, poor child, he had heard them repeating, in turn, in low voices, when they thought they were alone. But Nicola was never very far away, hiding behind a wall, behind the sofa, so that he would not be seen too much but not forgotten, either.

Sabina stopped insisting. She began reading again, resigned, but she didn't re-occupy the other half of the chair. Her eyes fell on an ad: "Advice to mothers of families!" it said, and then sang the praises of Phosphatine Falières, "the most highly recommended food for children." When her friends stopped nursing, they exchanged information on products like that. She would never have a newborn, but now she had a child, a son of her own. It was only a matter of time, sooner or later Nicola would stop hiding in the house like a wild animal and would yield to the love she had been preparing for him, ever since she and her husband had understood that the cradle would remain empty but not their hearts. When she decided to welcome one of the orphans of the tragedy, Giuseppe had warned her: "It won't be your imaginary son, it will be one of flesh and blood, and maybe you won't like him."

But Sabina liked Nicola immediately, with his hair that was too long and his dazed yet wary expression. He was an unusual and troubled child, but still a child. Maybe he didn't like her, and that was a painful uncertainty.

Attracted by the photos of a girl with a horse, she began reading an article on the life of some American women, cowgirls. Their freedom fascinated her, even though she would never have had the courage to wear men's clothing, to let herself be pictured without makeup.

Was a mother like this: nothing from which to protect himself, no one for whom to pretend; not a powder keg but a magic powder that dissolved obligations and fiction, a full warm embrace. With Sabina, Nicola would not be afraid. She waited for him, didn't force him, even to love her; she didn't interpret his thoughts, didn't put herself in his place, didn't insist on the opposite of what he really wanted.

Nicola approached the chair.

The magazine was open to a page that showed a woman in a cowboy hat, smiling and happy in an unusual way, out of the ordinary. He had never seen a woman like that. He had a great desire to read the caption, or, rather, to consume the whole article. He came a little closer.

Sabina looked up and gave him a big smile.

"Come," she repeated. "Come here and read with me." The space beside her was warm, inviting. From the magazine basket a ball of wool stuck out, every so often Sabina put down the magazines and began knitting. A thread of blue wool. She could bind him, as his old mother had done: it was an instantaneous vision, and Nicola ran away.

# THE MAGICIAN

*The first Arcanum—the principle underlying all
the other twenty-one Major Arcana of the Tarot—
is that of the rapport of personal effort and of
spiritual reality.*

No, I would not ingest potions or inject soaps into my body to
abort. I was cowardly, afraid of dying myself, of ending up like
the women who'd bled to death in the stories of abortionists and
their victims told by my grandmother to keep me from imprudent acts. And I was courageous out of recklessness, convinced
that, if the world was urging the people of Messina to be reborn,
no one could stigmatize a real birth. With the unconsciousness of
a survivor I said to myself that, if no man wanted me because I
had given birth to a child, then, too bad, I would remain alone:
as I would find bread for myself I would find it for two, at the
cost of stealing from the larders of others. Life had burdened me
with enough injustices, it was time for retribution. The freedom I
wanted, which the earthquake had given me, would confirm my
dishonor: because of that stain my father would definitively reject

me and I would have no more chains. Bitterly I had to admit that he was right. Desires have a price, he'd repeat when I asked him for something.

I asked Jutta to help me find Madame. I was entering into an unfathomable future and I needed a guide, I deserved a reading of the tarot: a second card would reveal how I would be able to feed and protect the child. I was also anxious to know if I would survive the birth, if the fetus was healthy, and if it resembled me, because it should have nothing to do with that sailor.

One night I dreamed that the *Morgana* set sail from Messina and was swallowed up by a black sky, while a warm sun of rebirth looked out from the coast. If it was a boy, would he be disgusting like his father? The question terrified me. Would that man ever return, would he look for me? His accent wasn't from the south, I couldn't identify it precisely, but as soon as he left the Strait he would no longer have a reason to come again, unless some politician decided to recall him to shower him with medals. A medal for volunteering in Messina and Reggio had now become a tool for putting oneself forward and getting ahead; I wouldn't be surprised if he, too, had ambitions. I hoped he had died in the collapse of a building, as he himself had feared. Would I see his eyes again in my child's eyes? Every time I thought of the sailor, two eyes with long lashes materialized, staring at me. Not knowing whose they were, I said to myself that they were my child's, but deep down I didn't believe it. In truth I was sure I had a girl inside me, and the idea calmed me, removed every fear. Then I said to myself: It will be a girl even if it's a boy.

Jutta, asking again and again in the city I no longer ventured out into, finally was able to get news of Madame: no help for it, she had returned to France, and while the king of Italy awarded medals to every soldier, the memory of the seer in the places of the disaster was erased; she was called a witch and no one wished to speak of her. It was the fate of women; I grieved. That night I dreamed I had the deck of tarot cards, I shuffled and cut them, but I saw no figure, the cards were white and empty, useless. I would have to get by on my own.

I didn't tell the sisters about my pregnancy. Some began to treat me with irritation, considering me fickle and proud, because I refused the food and in fact walked away from it; meat and fish gave me nausea. Instead I eagerly ate scraps and side dishes, like the *minestra sabbaggia*, the soup of wild herbs seasoned with oil, to which I added an abundance of salt because it lessened the metallic taste I always had in my mouth and the excess saliva that forced me to spit secretly. Rosalba stopped along the roadside to pick sorrel leaves and borage for me, Jutta got the pot ready, and Mother Fortunata gave us ugly looks because I'd fill my dish two or three times with this and ignore the rest.

In February the government declared that the state of siege on the Strait was over. A few days later, Rosalba said to Jutta and me that the Superior had summoned them. The order had assigned them to a destination: some would remain in Sicily, others leave for the continent. As long as it was a matter of first aid, it was tolerable that a group of nuns should live outdoors, in a camp, but it was now time to find each nun a proper and protected solution. The camp would be emptied, and Jutta and I would be abandoned to our capacity to invent a life for ourselves.

I was seized by fear, rather than uncertainty. I hadn't gone out for weeks; with the excuse of being the servant in our camp I saw no other souls but the sisters. I feared the crowd, I feared walking in a new city, which I had left in smoke and would find again deserted, I feared not recognizing it, I feared having to confront all my memories at once: the years before and the days of the fire. No matter how I looked at it, I wasn't ready for the future.

"Barbara," Sister Rosalba resumed, "I'm sorry to leave you, but it's better this way. Not everyone here looks kindly on your sin."

So the sisters had found me out? And Rosalba, with whom I had never talked about it, how did she know I was pregnant? Jutta, it must have been she who betrayed me.

"No one told me," Rosalba explained. "My Barbara, we understand that in that body you are two. Just because we're nuns we're not ignorant of the world. I've seen sisters with full bellies, have you never heard of babies born in convents? And how many are not born. I asked Jutta how to help you, but she denied that you were expecting a child, she loves you, trust her. And don't trust anyone else, the rumors about you have become malicious."

My secret was the favorite subject of the camp.

"I asked for a place for you in the Regina Elena village. A pregnant woman will always find a roof over her head. You have to go right away to where the queen has ordered the church to be built. There's a priest who is assigning the new lodgings, you're already on the list. I had to choose a name for you, and since I'm about to go to Calabria, near Cosenza, I thought of Barbara Cosentino. That way no one will recognize you, you're a different person."

"You said I'm pregnant?" Shame at my condition was stronger than my amazement at a sister who lied so casually.

"And that you lost your husband in the disaster. You're not at the end of the third month, right? I said Cosentino was the name of your husband, they won't ask you any other questions."

"But it's known that I'm not married."

Rosalba laughed. "You have in your mind the city of before. The records have been destroyed, families no longer exist. No one knows anyone, and if people do recognize each other they pretend not to, it suits everyone. Criminals have taken the clothes of respectable individuals and the houses of the dead, gentlemen reduced to hunger have become thieves, streetwalkers cool themselves with elegant fans stolen from ladies' trunks, and mothers of families become prostitutes to get food for their children. In Messina you're no longer who you are but who you can and want to be."

"And if I meet my father?"

"You have a treasure in your belly, use it: the wives of the dead have precedence over all, like war widows. There's a place for Jutta, too: she'll have to help you bring up this poor child who lost its father before it was born. Your father won't help you."

Looking at Jutta I understood that she and Rosalba had already talked about this, which was the best solution, the only one, but I was still afraid.

The next day we packed our bags, mine was almost empty, I put in it the book by Matilde Serao that I'd read a hundred times, the fragment of writing from the tombstone of Letteria Montoro and her flaking photograph, plus a couple of changes of clothes.

Sister Velia pointed to a pile of garments. "They're a large size, they'll be useful to you," and I took them and didn't lower my eyes. I was no longer ashamed of the creature who was saving me: I will give life, what do you have of equal importance to set against me, besides your scorn?

Mother Fortunata didn't come to say goodbye, she had us informed that she was busy taking care of correspondence, and urged us to pray a lot and never forget to thank God for our good luck. Again my breath failed; now it wasn't the child but, rather, the terror of returning among people.

A last glance at the crucifix hanging at the head of my cot, and those weeks, too, were behind me.

# THE SUN

*[T]he Arcanum "The Sun" with which we are occupied is an Arcanum of children bathing in the light of the sun. Here it is not a matter of finding occult things, but rather of seeing ordinary and simple things in the light of day of the sun—and with the look of a child.*

Every afternoon, Sabina sat in the green velvet armchair and pulled out of the straw basket a copy of her favorite magazine, *La Donna*. Soon afterward, Nicola would look into the living room, she would raise her head and beckon him to come in with a gesture of her chin, but he never sat with her. Gradually Sabina began to buy other magazines, news reports, weeklies, including *Giornalino della Domenica*. Seeing it, Nicola reacted with a smile and hurried to take it from her, so she understood it was his favorite.

They always had something new to read; to become mother and child, Sabina and Nicola used that silent appointment, and he began to sit at her feet, but always warily. He kept an eye on the balls of wool in the basket and the titles of the journals.

One afternoon, his curiosity about an article on the oldest, most unusual Piedmontese pastry shops was so great that Nicola came closer than usual, almost touching Sabina. She pretended indifference, but inside she was trembling, and observed the child's interest. When she realized that it was fading, because he had read the whole article and stopped looking at the images, she quickly turned the page. A photo appeared of Vittorio Emanuele III, standing on a pile of ruins in Messina. The title said: "*Sicilian-Calabrian Earthquake: Brothers, we have not forgotten you.*" Sabina started, at last the space beside her was filled by a small warm body. Nicola had perched there, his eyes fixed on the page. The sovereign extended his arms over the city in a gesture that was intended to be protective, but he resembled a victor rather than a man stunned by disaster.

"I'm sorry," Sabina apologized, afraid that the article would disturb the child and she could lose that contact, and she hugged Nicola tight against her.

He would have liked to extend the margins of the photo disproportionately, widen it to expand the view and see the city as it had become, as he had imagined it when he was about to step onto its streets and then had returned to the torpedo boat to protect the unknown girl.

"Did you go there often?" Sabina crept into that crack, Nicola's past was a dense, dark place, defended by impenetrable barricades.

He thought of the August holiday when he had gone with Maria and Vincenzo to the procession of the Vara, of how his mother had elbowed her way in to get the holy ropes, rejoicing obscenely as she grabbed them. He thought of the ferry crossing, of Maria quivering with excitement to get home with the booty in her pocket, while Vincenzo, looking over the parapet, smoked.

"If you don't feel like talking about it that doesn't matter, did you see I also got you the latest *Giornalino*?" Sabina quickly changed the subject, but Nicola had stayed there, on the Strait.

He was in the devastated city glimpsed as he was disembarking from the *Morgana*, he had followed the Messinese woman with dark curly hair, blinded by thirst. How had her life continued, how did she spend her days? Sooner or later he would meet her again, and maybe Sabina and Giuseppe would adopt her, too.

"Would you like to go away, take a trip the three of us? I've thought of a very strange place, as far as possible from where you were born, exactly the opposite."

The journey before Biella had been the one from Reggio to Messina and back, quick and terrible. And the last person he had spoken to was the sailor who had asked him for the silver. While Nicola observed the violence against the girl, everything inside him screamed, but not even a whisper had come out of him. Since then he'd had no voice.

"What do you say, shall we go?" Sabina insisted. Nicola nodded. A journey to the future was what he needed, a journey that would cancel those pasts, the grim trips on the ferry and the black recollection of memories deposited against his will. He grabbed the *Giornalino della Domenica* and became absorbed in a new serial story.

Before departing, the three Crestanis went to Turin to do some special shopping: jackets for snow, shoes and bathrobes, heavy pajamas, supplies of liqueurs and chocolates. Three fur-lined hats, the same but in different sizes and colors: blue for Giuseppe, white for Sabina, yellow for Nicola.

Nicola's size and measurements increased, the flesh pulled on the sleeves of the jackets and the pant legs. His hair, kept short and neat, grew quickly, and he always needed a trim. As they were going to the shops under the porticoes, the parents noticed a sign, "Gentlemen's Barber," and decided to leave the child.

"When should we come and get him?" Giuseppe asked. Sabina meanwhile helped Nicola arrange the cape over his shoulders. It was the first time they'd been separated, but it would be a short separation, less than half an hour.

Nicola stared attentively at his reflection in the gold-framed mirror: his cheeks had filled out, his face lengthened. He had more chin, more ears. It was as if the wind of the North had smoothed out the tension of his nervous features. The stool he was sitting on was high, but Nicola touched the floor with his feet: either the barbers of Piedmont had different measurements from those of Reggio or he had grown.

While the scissors quickly grazed his neck, his nape, his ears, he reviewed the changes of the past weeks. At night he went to sleep with a mother, in the morning he woke with breakfast in bed brought by a father, and he spent the days with a teacher for literature, a teacher for mathematics, and a teacher for piano.

At first Sabina and Giuseppe had sent Nicola to school, but the children were mean to him: they called him "the mute Calabrese" and made fun of him. Nicola endured in silence. The teachers had talked to the Crestanis, and in the end they had decided to shelter that child who had suffered so much already.

"Have you ever been to Milan?" Sabina had asked him a few days earlier, and the answer was no.

"Or the Valle d'Aosta? And the mountains? Have you ever heard the sound that a glacier makes at night? Or slept in a mountain hut?"

No, no, no. Nicola had shaken his head. About the past, his answers didn't vary. Until December 1908, Nicola had done nothing apart from endure.

"You're sure you'd like to go to the mountains?" Sabina had repeated, to be sure she wasn't doing something against his will, something that would make him feel uneasy. His new mother's tone was the opposite of Maria's: a tender and welcoming glide, where it was easy to agree and nod.

About the future the answer was always yes, yes, yes. The future knocked and insisted, carrying with it all the colors of the world.

While the barber dried his hair, Nicola reached for a magazine and, leafing through it, came upon another article about the earthquake, full of disputes about what had happened in the days following. Should it be called an earthquake or a tidal wave? Had the first ships to arrive been the Russians or the English? Which of the armed forces had been most kind and caring during the rescues? Was it true that Prime Minister Giolitti, learning in the early hours of the morning of the destruction of Messina and Reggio Calabria, had reacted with irritation at the southerners, who exaggerated everything? True that a woman had given birth amid the rubble, the labor pains accelerated by the shocks and fear? Was Queen Elena's compassion sincere, or was her sorrow propaganda to cover the king's insensitivity? The anonymous author commented on the same photo of Vittorio Emanuele III that Nicola had already seen, writing that the hands of the sovereign had been modified so that he would seem to be making a charitable gesture, but in reality he had had them in his pockets, which wasn't surprising, since he was mainly interested in money. On the next page, in corroboration, you could see the original photo: even the king's expression seemed harsher, indifferent. Nicola had never read anything like that: Could one speak of the king in such a manner? The article went on to question the heroism of the soldiers, of whatever nationality, and implying that rapes and thefts had been covered up by a patina of medals.

Disturbed, he closed the magazine quickly, with the sensation of having stuck his nose in something mistaken and forbidden. On the cover was the word "anarchy": Nicola remembered that during a sermon, in Reggio Calabria, the priest had said anarchy was a manifestation of the Devil.

"How handsome you look with that new hair!" Sabina's trilling voice and the sound of the glass door opening brought him back to reality.

# THE STAR

*The light-force which emanates from the star—
constituted through the marriage of contemplation
with activity, and which is the antithesis of the
thesis that "there is nothing new under the sun"—
is hope. It proclaims to the world: "What has been
is that which prepares what will be, and what has
been done is that which prepares what will be
done; there is only that which is new under the
sun. Each day is a unique event and revelation
which will never be repeated."*

My dear Barbara,

It's as if I were writing to you from the future: I've just left our earthquake-ravaged land and am in Cosenza, where there was also an earthquake, but three years ago. That is, I am in the situation you will be in three years from now, or: nothing will change.

I walk along the street and it seems to me that I am still there with you. One has only to look at what happened here to understand that the time it takes for reconstruction will be very different from what you're told. Many stores have not reopened. Some towns, like Aiello, live with the terror of a rib of rock that might come free again and crush them. Those who have lost family and home have nothing, no compensation or anything else, despite the fact that there was a lot of talk at the time and a competition to see who could be more generous with the Calabrian sisters and brothers. Does it remind you of something? But I don't want to put you in a bad mood. The human spirit doesn't change, but God will be merciful with you, I know it, I feel it, it can only be thus.

I'm well, I have a decent room in the convent, the sisters call me "the earthquake victim" and spoil me a little too much. And yet I miss our days, I even miss the encampment, our understanding one another beyond words.

Give me your news. How is it in the village of the queen? Is Jutta well, are people kind to you? Do you have enough to eat? Has the nausea stopped? The baby is growing? When it's possible I'll come and see you, I promise.

I think of you with all my affection, give Jutta a kiss for me, too.

Yours ever,

Rosalba

Calling the cabin assigned to Jutta and me in the Regina Elena village home was excessive, but Rosalba's letters were breaths of fresh air, and, compared to the way we camped after the disaster, the new lodgings appeared more than comfortable. The reality, however, was different.

Although the saga of rebirth insisted on a row of small modern-style houses, which we were asked to pose in front of for the official photographs, the structures were unstable and precarious, full of drafts and loved by ants and mice. At night we were afraid: the doors swung back and forth in the wind gusts, and the sensation of being tolerated by the community did not correspond to a concrete sense of protection; the day's appearances were belied by the night's desperation. Two cabins down from ours a man waited for darkness to get drunk on mysterious reserves of alcohol, and we heard him beating his wife, banging fists and sticks against the walls. One morning I tried to talk to the woman, but received in response a snarl and an invitation to mind my own business. Jutta, approaching her at Mass, had told her that we could make space in our cabin for her and her child; the answer had arrived in a dialect so thick and loud that there was no doubt it was a curse. We no longer mingled: The atmosphere among the cabins was one of unassailable distrust. All of us held tight to the little we had, and a violent husband wasn't the worst that could happen.

In the morning we got up early, went to claim our ration of food, muttered about where the aid money had ended up, and grumbled about when the promised houses would be ready, in the other villages as well as in ours; they were being constructed with money from foreigners, and so Messina, once the glorious commander, was named like a group of colonies: the Swiss village, the American village, and then mine, the village of the inevitable sovereign Elena, also a colony.

"Don't you want to leave here?" I asked Jutta on one of those afternoons of sun without a season, typical of our land. "Don't you want to get your house back?"

After months, the excuse of waiting to find out if the friend and the maid were miraculously alive no longer held up. Construction had begun in the ruins of what had fallen, and if there were dead people under the new foundations, too bad: the city would be reborn on the corpses.

"I don't think you've understood. I don't have a house."

I put aside the book by Matilde Serao, which I was rereading.

"I have money, yes, in a bank, and that's why I'm here. It's not much, but we can live on it until we find work."

"And the house where you lived with your husband?"

"When the baby was born dead, the marriage died, too. We no longer slept together. I knew he had a lover, but I didn't know who she was, or that they'd had two daughters. I discovered it when I opened the will. That was why he'd stopped repeating that not having children was the greatest misfortune of his life—because he had them. He didn't marry that other woman out of respect for me, but he left the house to the daughters, to apologize for not having been present. To me he wrote a letter in which he wished me the best, but I would have to manage on my own."

"That's horrible!"

"Men. They can't make up their minds, they're afraid of doing harm and do worse. They live on the edge, and when they die they leave a mess."

"So you came to Sicily to put all that behind you."

"And also because, once, I was happy here."

We were made of flesh, bones, and nerves. We were made of ourselves and nothing else, kept alive by a creature with different blood that was nourished on mine and swelled my belly; every morning I woke up bigger and gained greater respect and credibility. I got used to introducing myself as the widow Cosentino, I settled inside that name fully, determined to take advantage of the possibilities and use it as a passport.

The nausea didn't go away, and in the morning Jutta massaged my back with a lotion for joint pain. More than once I was frightened by seeing blood in my feces, but my friend calmed me: It's normal, she repeated, tilting her head to one side. The priest sent a doctor to examine me, a lean man with a gloomy, mean expression and breath that smelled of death. He reproached me for the poverty of my diet, then looked at Jutta fiercely and ordered her to make me eat meat at least three meals a week: You want to kill this child? he thundered. And also: He'll be born among women, without substantial food how can he become a male?

With an entire week's shopping money, we bought some very good, very tender fillet. I asked Jutta to cook it thoroughly, but after I swallowed a few forced mouthfuls my stomach couldn't keep it down, and the fillet brought up with it the lunch of a few hours before.

We never again spoke that doctor's name, although we told the priest that the pregnancy was proceeding wonderfully thanks to his advice. I threw up secretly, in the house, muffling the sound for fear someone would hear me.

In fact, there wasn't much money, and we had to find work. Jutta was no longer interested in biology; she said she would take the opportunity to change her life. At the parish church two women from the village were teaching a course in dressmaking to those who didn't have a job; we both went to the first lesson, but I wasn't good at it, I cut myself, pricked myself, and, because of my belly, struggled to stay in my chair. Jutta gave me a withering look. I knew what she thought, and I agreed: crossing my legs under me as I was doing would twist the fetus and the child would be born deformed.

I went reluctantly to the second meeting, wondering what I was doing there. Jutta, on the other hand, was completely absorbed, and didn't even notice when, after barely half an hour, I sneaked out to breathe a little freedom.

"You don't want to work?"

The priest's voice surprised me.

"You need to learn a trade. You can't remain idle."

"I don't like sewing."

"What do you like?"

"Reading," I answered impulsively, "but it's not a trade."

"And you know how to write, no?"

"I don't know. I've never written. Not yet . . ." I answered in confusion.

"You filled out the documents and signed them in front of me the morning I gave you the house."

Writing didn't mean only creating pages of literature, in fact mainly it meant making marks on a page, not being illiterate. I struggled to disconnect the two meanings of the word, but he was right.

"Yes, yes, of course."

"Come with me."

The only time I'd been alone with a man was on the torpedo boat, but I couldn't say no to the village priest, the person who had given me a house, whom I lied to every day by answering when he called me Signora Cosentino. I followed him to a cabin where no one lived yet; before entering I breathed hard and touched my stomach. Don't worry, said the voice of my baby from somewhere in my body: I believed it and stopped worrying.

"Here we can have up to forty children. Now, we won't find forty certainly, at most fifteen or twenty will come, the ones who aren't hiding. Some have never been to school. Some others will know many things, not from studying. Once they've seen an earthquake, children know everything."

Twenty desks stared at us, empty. Where did they come from? For a long time now I hadn't gone out into the city; so the schools had been abandoned, to be reconstructed in new places?

"Only the teacher is missing. You've studied, you've been to school, Signora Cosentino?"

I had been taught at home, but I nodded.

"I know you like books. It's clear, and you just confirmed it. Your friend seems to know about science, even though for now she's taken with sewing."

"I've never brought up a child . . . I don't know anything about children."

"You'll have to learn."

"I didn't like that doctor you sent me."

"What did he do to you?" The priest was alarmed.

"He treated me badly. I know what to do, I don't need someone to come and scold me."

"I'm sorry. I thought he could be helpful. But of course women have been making children since the dawn of time, the Virgin Maria teaches that you can make them by yourself, you don't need us," he smiled. I smiled in return. "Even if that doesn't please my colleagues. You know what the truth is? For your condition we need a woman doctor, one who's studied medicine: I know someone in Catania, but here it's more difficult. It was already difficult to find a man. The doctors have fled Messina. As long as there were the wounded of the emergency it was one thing, but now there's neither money nor glory."

"Find me a midwife, that will be useful."

"And you'll come and teach the children?"

I didn't know what to say. In my family the women had never worked, my great-grandmother the seamstress wasn't paid in money: to have a trade was unseemly, her passion was tolerated as a pastime. I thought of her, 'a maestra: at that precise moment Jutta was learning her art; I, instead, would steal her nickname. Together we would honor her memory, fulfilling it by turns.

"When do you want me to start?"

"Tomorrow morning at eight the children will be here, I'll take care of paper and ink, also books. Tell me if you need anything, but anyway I'll be here. I'll pay you with money from the benevolent fund."

"I might not be good at teaching."

"You have a child in your womb, you're getting along by yourself, and I trust your smile. I don't need anything else."

Outside Cabin 19, the sun was brighter than it had been in all the springs of my life.

# THE JUDGMENT

*Thus, the last judgment will be essentially the experience by mankind of awakened conscience and completely restored memory.*

The carriage transporting the Crestani family was ascending, climbing upward, proceeding solemnly in the snow. Nicola leaned out the window to observe the glittering white blanket that until then he had seen only in the exotic drawings of travel magazines. Sharp peaks pierced the sky, the clouds came closer, and the child, wrapped in the warmth of a thick coat, hat pulled down over his ears, his feet safe in padded shoes, felt the intoxication of one cold point on his warm body, a sliver of ice on the tip of his nose. His cheeks were reddened by the tingling mountain air.

"The chalet is close," Sabina said with a caress that was also a way of pulling him back in, a gesture of love that hid her worry that, leaning out, he might lose his balance. Chalet, mountain hut: the words that had flooded Nicola's imagination acquired real outlines. The brown of the houses, the milky clouds, the white of the glaciers: every color reminded him how black life in Reggio had been.

And yet on the Strait Nicola had seen rainbows after the rain, had dodged the yellow light of spring, had wandered in the sparkle of sudden bright spells in winter, when the air was cold—not as cold as in Valle d'Aosta—and the sky clear. The whole sun could lie easily in the sky of Reggio Calabria, while in the valleys there were too many mountain curves interrupting the horizons.

After the last turn, the carriage stopped.

The chalet had a gable roof and wood shingles, windows with white grates. Nicola was startled: it was like the houses in the Swiss village that had arisen in Messina after the earthquake. He had seen photos of it in an article, and by now he was looking for such articles with increasing curiosity, focused always on the same question: Where did the girl of the *Morgana* live? Every photograph was a piece of the puzzle, every description a clue. At night, before going to sleep, he imagined her walking through Messina, then closing the door of the house behind her: one time the house was a cabin in the American village, near the offices and the banks, another it was in the middle of Queen Elena, willed by the sovereign. Since he had started looking for news of Messina and Reggio, he knew everything about the reconstruction. Now it was natural for him to think of her in a chalet in the Swiss village, made up of small foreign cottages like the ones the donors inhabited in their own country.

The Valle d'Aosta, Nicola discovered, getting out of the carriage that had brought them there, resembled Switzerland, and since he wanted to assume for himself and the girl a parallel fate, he couldn't help seeing her enter a house like his, at that precise moment. And if it wasn't so? Who could say where visions and dashed hopes ended up if they deteriorated over time like an unsuccessful spread of tarot cards, like a wrong card from Madame. And Madame, what had happened to her? Nicola didn't know what to wish for her. Collecting articles on the apocalypse of the Strait, he had discovered many interesting facts about fortune tellers and diviners: it seemed that in the weeks before December 28th there had been unmistakable signs. A woman had entered the court in Messina, beside herself because her son had been condemned, and cried that an earthquake "with eyes" would come, that it would see, and identify, the guilty and the evil who deserved it, and would aim at them alone, in order to save those who were good. The archbishop of Reggio Calabria had died shortly before, having written that luckily he would not witness the destruction of the city. After the catastrophe, almost everyone had a premonition, a foreboding to recount to the journalists, whether it was a warning that came from the body of the blessed Eustochia in Messina or a tongue twister that had unfortunately appeared in the issue of a magazine—but then, Nicola continued to wonder, how blind were those who had suspected nothing? Those who hadn't seen an anomalous dip in the sea or noticed the dark atmosphere, the ochre-colored air "typical of earthquakes"? Those who, like him, were too caught up in protecting themselves and saving their lives daily to have the time and the astuteness to fantasize on other fronts, about other dangers.

"Nicola, let's go in now, it's too cold," Giuseppe called him, a hint of exasperation staining his kindness.

He had waited while Nicola was absorbed in his thoughts, in front of the chalet, always careful not to force him, respecting his ongoing strange behavior. Nicola again promised himself to be a better son for that father who was freezing outside there, who had carried in the suitcases and in reproaching him seemed rather to reproach himself for being unable to do otherwise.

"You've never heard anything like it in the world, nothing is like the sound of a glacier," Sabina said, pulling up Nicola's blankets.

"The pieces of ice crack and separate during the night, and that sound is elegiac and monstrous, it doesn't resemble any form of living being," Giuseppe had told him one afternoon. "I was here for the first time as a child, with my parents, and now it's my turn to bring my son," he added, and to Nicola it seemed that his eyes were wet with emotion.

What was it like, then, this glacier? You had to keep from sleeping at any cost, or you might not hear anything. Nicola tried to stay awake as long as he could, but the journey had been tiring; he could no longer feel his legs because he'd been sitting for so long, and sleep soon had the better of him.

He dreamed of the cats that pursued him in Reggio Calabria, the same two of that final night, the bloody one and the wounded, but they had both become gentle, tame. They looked at him without meowing, and he had a desire to touch them. Then sleep was interrupted by a series of light vibrations, they came from something that was exploding, the sound of bubbles being pricked with a toothpick. After that, creaks, roars, sonorous avalanches descending from the valleys intermittently broke the silence.

That was it, the glacier. Yes, it was majestic and frightening at the same time, Nicola was gripped by fear, he got up suddenly and bolted to his parents' bed.

Sabina and Giuseppe welcomed him as if they'd been expecting him. In the warmth, between them, Nicola thought he had never been able to react to the night by fleeing, when his wrists were bound by ropes and his bed was a bier in the depths of a distant cellar. Now there were no ropes, no cuts on his skin, nothing kept him from asking for help and shouting his fear, he could appear fragile without being punished, ignored, or mocked.

Sabina breathed softly, Nicola huddled against her. Before falling asleep again he asked God not to give him anything more than what he already had, that love would be enough forever. Only, please, he added, don't let there be any more earthquakes. At most one "with eyes," which would continue to exterminate the wicked and save the three of them.

The next morning Nicola awakened to find a tray on the bed. A plate with a slice of cake, apple pancakes, fruit syrup. A glass of hot water. A cup that he uncovered immediately, anxious to discover what good thing it was hiding. The aroma, the color, and the consistency were unmistakable: hot chocolate. The same as at Caffè Spinelli, in the room dense with smoke, spices, and the scent of Fera bergamot, which the women of Reggio Calabria sprinkled on their coats, giving Nicola the impression that they all went around with his family pasted onto them. The hot chocolate of winter afternoons, rare oases of serenity, while Maria was distracted and he could enjoy in peace something he really liked. Beside it, the most recent issue of the *Giornalino della Domenica*. Nicola opened it, ready to give in to a comfortable happiness, and began reading the new episode of *Cadetti di Guascogna*, and then he moved on to an article about Easter celebrations. The sweets typical of every part of Italy were listed, and immediately Nicola looked for Calabria, finding the recipe for *cudduraci*, pastries in the shape of rings with two or three hard-boiled eggs set into them. Vincenzo ordered them every year for Sunday breakfast. Nicola liked to take out the eggs and eat them right away, and then scrape the pieces of shell off the cookie and eat it by itself. He turned the page again. "The Heroes Who Saved the Children of the Earthquake" was the title of a photographic essay. His hands trembled and he felt a shock to his heart. There were six pictures of sailors, six closeups, twelve eyes, six heads of hair. The fourth was him, the man from the *Morgana*.

Sabina entered and saw her son in tears.

"I didn't want coming here to have this effect," she said in alarm, but Nicola didn't stop. "It's my fault, I'm sorry." Sabina saw the *Giornalino* open to the article about the heroes of the earthquake, closed it abruptly and threw it far away. "I have to be more careful about what you read." She began to cry, too.

Nicola stopped. No, he shook his head. He had to tell her that she had nothing to do with it.

"It's my fault, I don't know how to be a mother," she sobbed.

No, no, no, Nicola shook his head in vain, unable to console her.

"I don't want the Devil to come and get me!"

Sabina stopped, stunned. Was that her son's voice? The ancient and powerful voice of a creature who has traversed a thousand eras and a hundred lives resounded in her ears and in her breast.

"No devil will come," she said, trying to soothe him.

"Off the ship, off the ship!"

"Sweetheart, we're in the mountains, there's no sea here."

Sabina went over to Nicola to hug him, but she bumped the breakfast tray, which fell off the bed. The cup with the chocolate broke, and Nicola turned to look at the shards on the floor.

"It doesn't matter. We'll take care of it later," Sabina soothed him.

"We'll take care of it later," Nicola repeated, amazed. His tone now was a child's. The window glass was steamed up by the warm air of the stove and by the snow.

It was thus, in the shadow of the glacier, that Sabina heard from her son the story of what he had seen on the torpedo boat. She listened with a stab of pain for the secret he had carried inside him, and was upset with herself: How had she been able to concentrate exclusively on the earthquake, without considering the days of solitude that had followed? A child of eleven, suddenly alone in the world. A world of men against which he had no defenses.

"Poor girl," she murmured. And also: "You'll see, she managed, we women are strong, don't you think about it anymore, don't you think about it anymore, don't think about it."

Nicola fell into her arms and slowly it all grew distant, while Sabina kissed his hair, his forehead, his hands.

Soon afterward, Giuseppe entered the room thinking he'd find them absorbed in reading. Nicola and Sabina instead were sleeping, next to each other. He felt extraneous to the scene, to the intimacy of that room, and was about to leave.

"Lie down here with Mamma and me," said the voice of his son unexpectedly.

# TEMPERANCE

*What is the message of the Angel with two wings,
in the red and blue robe, holding two vases, one
red and one blue, and making water gush in a
mysterious way from one vase to the other? Is he
not the one who bears the good news that beyond
the duality of "either-or" there is—or is possible—
still that of "not only-but also" or "both-and"?*

The Church was watching over us. So they all said, and Jutta and
I repeated it mockingly, sitting on the straw chairs in front of our
cabin, alluding to the freedom with which you could now circum-
vent the rules, as the odor of the soup on the fire wouldn't stay
inside, but came to us outside and saturated our shawls.

The sun set little by little before our eyes, which no longer saw
the Strait, for in between there were so many ruins that by now
I had forgotten I lived on the sea. April, arriving, brought Easter
and demolished the days of Lent. At the end of March, the wind
from the north had knocked on our bones, forcing us to knot our
shawls tighter. Jutta insisted: Cover up, cover up. In fact I never

felt cold with my belly, the growing child was my stove, I sweated, and the armpits of my dresses stank. I had to wash them often and the soap wore them thin, until they were threadbare around the elbows or collar.

"The Church has watched over us again," Jutta laughed, while we were sitting in front of the cottage stealing the last light of afternoon. "The third wedding in a week."

"Who is it this time?"

"Rosa's daughter and Carlo, the baker."

"Another bun in the oven." I had become more vulgar. I wasn't ashamed of laughing noisily, speaking in a loud voice, making remarks on subjects I would once have ignored: yet another effect of the pregnancy, that symptomatic dictatorship of the body that made me see in a different light the bodies of others, of all other men. And of all other women.

As if the walls of the cabins were transparent, I passed through them and spied on the girls: at night they made love, flashed like lightning in a storm, kindled fires in the darkness. Disobey was the word that enabled them to survive; the mothers endured, and hurried to celebrate their daughter's marriage before the sin was evident. I liked those young women: what for my body had been violence they knew how to get with the joy of rebellion; and even if they had to bow their heads like thieves, they were courageous, daring.

Thanks to them, my child would have in the village many sisters and brothers, many cousins, as long as we stayed there; the time of the births would arrive, but how long would the time of reconstruction last? The survivors coupled with one another, the future was promises forgotten by the rulers, vague promises left to gather dust along with the pile of magazines that every so often Jutta and I remembered to throw away: Messina will be reborn more beautiful, Messina rises again, new plans for Messina.

"How did it go today?" Jutta changed the subject. She got up to pull the shawl tight over my chest, which was gradually getting bigger; under the dress my nipples darkened and spread.

It had been a difficult day. Mimma, the wildest and most unruly of my students, had broken a window in an attempt to sneak out of the room, taking advantage of a moment when I had left to arrange with the priest for the delivery of some chairs.

She was a tempestuous child. I knew that, like many of them, she had lost her father in the earthquake. Each had a different reaction to loss: there were some who talked a lot and some not at all, some who shielded themselves by studying diligently and some whose exorcism was boasting. Mimma had a demagogic tendency; she was very smart and refused to cooperate with her companions, preferring to show off in startling actions. She had been hurt falling out the window, and, after scolding her, I told her to come to school the next morning with her mother.

Jutta said she wouldn't even know where to begin to keep those unknown children under control. They arrived in class in disarray, like dishes scattered on a table, and making them work together was a continuous effort. It was difficult to give dictation to the young ones while the older children wrote summaries; not to assign grades that emphasized the disparities; and to make them want to return the next day. Just keeping them in school was difficult, as everything they'd learned in recent months had been outside of school, outside of their homes, and outside of themselves as well. Keeping them inside, while they still felt the call of the outside. I was about to ask her about her day, about the dressmaking course that was now advanced, when we were interrupted.

"So I'm right, you're *'a maestra*."

Standing before us was Elvira, my grandmother's neighbor who had lost her daughters the night of the earthquake. She stared at us with one hand on her hip, her head tilted, and the expression of someone who had come to look for us in particular.

"Mimma described you well—you emerged precisely from her words. I made her repeat your name twice because it didn't fit. When I knew you, your name wasn't the widow Cosentino."

"What do you have to do with Mimma?"

"She's my daughter."

That girl was one of Elvira's daughters? She didn't look like her, and then: How could she have survived? In the collapse of our part of the Palazzata no one had remained alive. I myself had asked repeatedly, I had asked Jutta to ask, and the answer was always the same: No one but us. Neither my grandmother nor Jutta's friend or maid. No one.

"You found her?" I asked, confused.

"We all found something. You, in fact, a husband . . ."

Jutta stood up. "Signora, if you've come to threaten us, you can go back to where you came from."

"What do I care about threatening you? I learned to get by in these months, which maybe before I wasn't able to do."

Behind the hard, challenging expression a strained face was revealed. Elvira had a wish to cry, her desire to break down vibrated, so I freed a seat from the sewing that Jutta was practicing; but she refused to sit down. A gust of wind gave her an excuse to cover her eyes with her hands.

"If you stay, besides the soup I can make three egg frittatas with Gruyère. Do you like the cheese from the north?" Jutta must have had the same sensation, because she immediately softened. "Unfortunately we can't have meat, if you sit down with us we'll tell you why."

"I have to return to the American village."

"We'll just keep you a moment, but at least don't eat alone."

A few minutes later, we had dragged the chairs inside and were all three sitting around the table. Jutta rose often to stir the soup and fry the eggs according to her recipe.

"They did it to me as well," said Elvira, staring at my belly. "And I wasn't lucky, no."

"What do you mean?"

"I didn't get pregnant, nothing remained to me, only the disgust."

I remembered clearly the two men in uniform who had approached at the dawn of the disaster, when we were still stunned. I remembered the way they had looked at her, and how I had tried in vain to carry her away, while she was ready for anything in the mad hope of having her daughters back.

"I wish I'd had a *picciriddu*, but I got nothing; instead, with the new year my husband showed up. His lover was dead, only he and one of their children had survived. I hated him, but the child had something in her eyes."

"You did well," I said. The gaze of a child: something that subjugated me, too, a specter I knew well. Since I had gotten off the torpedo boat *Morgana*, the eyes with the long lashes had continued to torment me. I set aside the shadow of my ghost and returned to reality. It must have been horrible to share a bed with a man like that.

"I did well, yes, because he died after a week. The earthquake had split his head from the inside, and his brain was bleeding, even if you couldn't see anything. Cerebral hemorrhage, but in those days, with all those who were bleeding on the outside, no one cared about the wounded without wounds. He died in front of me, and I'll tell you the truth: luckily I didn't have time to call the doctor because I don't know if I would have, and if I hadn't called I'd burn in hell when I die. But he didn't deserve any doctor."

"And Mimma?"

"She's my daughter now. The Madonna sent her to me. She's crazy, you've seen her." She laughed. "Completely mad, like the one who brought her into the world and like her father, but I'm raising her and no one can take her away from me. I'll straighten her out little by little. She didn't want to go to school and yet she's come around, she likes Teacher Cosentino."

"She's clever, but she's so skittish I'm afraid she'll escape me through the window. It's good to send her to me in class, the other students are fond of her," I exaggerated to reassure her.

"My three were three angels, this one is different, but anyway she's mine."

"They've opened the new registry office, you can register her with your surname."

"I'll keep her with my husband's surname, that way they'll give me the pension and the house. I don't have to explain it to you."

I lowered my gaze.

Jutta brought the eggs to the table and the soup waited. The hot cheese formed a string, and before reaching our mouths it stretched and lengthened, we had to break it with our fingers; we set aside the silverware and began eating with our fingers, perching comfortably with our bare feet under our skirts, while night fell on us.

The next night, Elvira came back with Mimma. Together they came the day after, too. The day after that, Jutta and I had already made a bed for the two of them, because it was better for them not to go home in the dark, and it was convenient for Mimma to come to school with me in the morning; we were near the school and she could sleep a little longer. Sleeping longer calmed her, and in the morning she was less agitated; besides, she was no longer alone—there was me, there was Jutta, there was that creature in my belly whom she fantasized about playing with.

Before a week had passed Mimma and Elvira had moved in

with us. Where we'd been two we would be four and then five, unless they gave us our houses first, but by now we had stopped believing in them, the future would arrive sooner or later, like death, and in the meantime you had to live. Before leaving the American village, Elvira gave her cabin to another woman, one whom the bureaucracy had cut out and who slept where she could, and she kept for herself only the request for a home in the new workers' housing. Who knew where, who knew when.

Meanwhile, we kept one another company. Jutta improved in the kitchen and I had less nausea. I began to taste some flavors again, but my mouth remained metallic and after every meal the food rose like acid, though usually I was able to keep it down—I wasn't throwing up every day. One morning I woke with my belly sticking out, as if it had doubled during the night. Jutta and Elvira asked me: Is it kicking? I didn't feel anything, only gurgling, and I was afraid that the child had died or wasn't strong enough to live and move.

"As long as you're throwing up there's no need to worry," said Elvira. "Then you'll stop and the kicks will start."

I looked at her, puzzled. "Trust me," she said, "I've had three children."

"Four," I added, pointing to Mimma, and transformed the loss of the three others into the one who represented the future.

One afternoon Jutta returned from the course all excited: As she was leaving, some women had stopped her to commission some mending. She stayed up late and delivered the garments the next morning, receiving in exchange the first money earned from that work and, most important, orders for men's and women's clothes. Few among those living in the cabins could afford a real dressmaker, but all were tired of wearing the clothes stolen from the dead, always the same and saturated with the smell of the catastrophe, always too short or too large, belonging to the souls buried under our feet.

"You hear them," Jutta whispered to me at night. "They'll never forgive us for living on top of them."

Then she, too, usually so solid, gave in to weeping softly, clinging to my shoulder, and it was I who caressed her hair and told her that it would all be all right, comforted her, as by day she did with me. I brought her hand to my belly and little by little she calmed down, we fell asleep together, close under the covers, while Mimma and Elvira slept in the other bed, in an embrace.

But that night Jutta didn't weep. She began to work on her first man's jacket, made from a curtain.

"You've never had a desire to return home?"

The question emerged spontaneously the Thursday of Easter, while we were taking turns in front of the mirror, tying the veils under our chins before visiting the tombs.

"This is my home," Jutta answered, abruptly. I already knew that, and yet I was glad to hear her say it, and I promised myself that I wouldn't ask her again. In reality I wanted to get to her friendship with my grandmother, about whom I knew very little. When we talked about her it was Jutta who asked, listened; I held on to the special relationship I had as her granddaughter, and became gradually more possessive in memory; but I knew that the figure of my grandmother was not contained in the family role, and now that she was no longer here I wanted to imagine her in the life she had far from me.

Jutta said they'd met at a party at the house of a biology professor, a mutual friend. I smiled thinking how the university fascinated Grandmother, how happy she was whenever she could touch the edges of that world. Jutta described an ostentatious living room, chandeliers, silver, a party that was far removed from where we were now: an unbridgeable distance. Had the earthquake been lurking in the faults in the sea that surrounded the balconies, had the earth's desire to sweep us away already cracked our foundations?

"Is this OK?" Mimma brought us back to the present, she, too, standing in front of the mirror. I arranged the veil so that it covered her neck, the west wind was blowing and I was afraid she'd catch cold. I realized only afterward that it was the same care Jutta showed toward me: it was easy for us to take care of others, less easy to care for ourselves.

Elvira was waiting for us in the doorway. We set off, the four of us, in a procession for the Easter visit to the tombs, altars of grain and sprouts that guarded the Eucharist, the body of Christ. The *graniceddi* were small tombs that received not the end of the body but the miracle of the Resurrection, and were displayed in the city's churches on Holy Thursday. The tradition was to visit at least seven, like the sorrows of the Madonna; Elvira said that for her five were enough, the wounds of our Lord.

It was a long time since I'd walked through Messina. The time of my solitary crossings in the just-destroyed city, still bleeding and in flames, was distant: now everything was covered by a quiet normality, the rubble piled at the street corners was like the wings in the theater, while new shops took the stage, along with jerry-built shacks, renovated offices, and even some hotels for travelers passing through. We headed toward the churches spared by the disaster, recalling among ourselves those we would never see again. With my grandmother I'd always started with San Gregorio, which no longer existed; we started instead at Santissima Annunziata dei Catalani, went on to the new churches built in the past months, and ordered a lemonade in a cloister beside the old Santa Maria Alemanna, the most beloved church. I looked for a free kneeling stool and, amid incense and flowers, knelt to pray, when a hand was placed on my shoulder.

"Barbara," a woman I didn't recognize called me.

She was wearing a light sweater with ruching at the neck, from her lobes hung a pair of teardrop pearl earrings, a scarf framed a large face with small features and dark skin.

"You're alive, then. You don't recognize me? I'm Vittorio Trimarchi's mother."

"Of course, I'm sorry," I lied, startled.

"We saw each other on December 27th, at *Aida*."

"Of course, I remember," I lied again, my heart pounding, because I remembered only her son.

"He had come for you." I looked at her in amazement. "It was all he talked about. We had tickets for the night before, but he wanted to exchange them at any cost: Mamma, Signora Ruello's granddaughter will be there, he said, all pleased."

"Where is he?" I stammered.

"What sort of question is that?" She seemed angry, more than surprised. "They pulled him out three days later, too late. I didn't move from there, I talked to him, prayed, but they took forever and killed him."

A hand wrung my heart until it crushed it. "He ended like the professor . . ." I added, breathless.

"Who? Salvemini? Where are you living? The professor is alive, he lost wife, children, sister, but he's still among us. Of course, he fled Messina, he who could."

"I had different news," I explained.

"It was the first days, when no one understood anything." Vittorio's mother looked down at my belly. "Is it mine?"

I blushed.

"Is it my son's?"

"What do you mean? We had never seen each other before that night."

She looked at me doubtfully, grim. "He had absolutely seen you. I suspected he wasn't telling me the truth, and also I didn't really trust you, you came to the city too often. Why didn't you stay in your town?"

Someone reproached us, asking us to be silent, we were in a church, after all. A candle went out, other people entered, I looked for Jutta and Elvira, but they must have already left and probably were waiting for me: Mimma couldn't stay still for long.

"I have to go," I defied the mother of Vittorio Trimarchi, and she followed me out.

"I'll find you and take back my grandson," she hissed, while my friends hurried over to me. "It's mine and not yours, understand?" She began shouting, then insulted and spit at me. A group of people approached.

"You're crazy, leave us alone," shouted Elvira. Jutta had taken Mimma and me by the hand, and some bystanders intervened to calm the woman.

We hurried away. The wind whipped hands and ears, the belly-stove was no longer working, and as soon as we were home Jutta prepared compresses to ward off ear infections and a salve for my scraped and cracked knuckles. We were shocked and frightened, but we tried to talk about other things in order not to frighten Mimma. Elvira told her a fairy tale, the child continued asking who was that woman and wasn't satisfied by hearing us answer that we didn't know either.

That night we shut ourselves in the cabin. Elvira fell asleep right away, but Mimma came to Jutta and me. She couldn't sleep, so we put her between us and she calmed down. I had agitated dreams: Vittorio's mother pulled on my stomach with long, bony hands and detached it from my body with a knife, I cried for help, but my friends didn't come. I woke in tears, Mimma escaped to her mother's bed, and was welcomed, Jutta calmed me, insisting that no one would take my child, not then or ever.

At dawn, a thud woke me that came right from the womb. My baby had given its first kick.

# THE LOVERS

*Does one not hear, in contemplating the sixth Card of the Tarot, a voice which says: "I have found you," and another which says: "Those who seek me find me"?*

Dear Emma,

Finally your letter arrived, if it had been delayed I would have written again. I miss you, too, thanks for sending the photo, I imagined your new mamma just like that, with blond hair, while I didn't imagine that your papa was bald. Anyway he's very elegant. Monsignor Cottafavi was right, our perfect parents were somewhere waiting for us. I'm sorry that the right family for me is in Biella and yours in Naples, because otherwise maybe we'd go to the same school, who knows! In the photo Camilla's hair is very long; I go to the barber often and my hair is never uncombed the way it was when we met.

My best memory of Reggio Calabria is our friendship.

A letter also arrived from the document office in Reggio. It said that my old parents are dead. Two weeks after we left they recovered the bodies and buried them in the cemetery. One day I'll go and find

them and bring them a bouquet of chrysanthemums and orchids—
we didn't have relatives there, so I don't think anyone ever goes.

My new mamma told me something very sad. My house was
destroyed. It was dangerous and they blew it up, because no one
could live there, and in its place another one will be built. You
remember the cellar where we met? I used to sleep there. I left
all my things, but I miss only my collection of magazines. My
mamma Sabina applied to buy me the back issues, so I won't
mind so much not having mine. I hope another child takes them.
I wonder if they'll build above the cellar or if it will stay as it is
now, with the door open to the garden where you came to look for
me. Maybe it would be good for storing wine and oil.

Anyway, now that we have the documents, my parents can
actually adopt me. Every so often at night I dream that my old
parents come back to get me, but I want to stay here and I hold
tight to Mamma's dress.

My old mother was the Devil, and also my father. I never told
you, because when we met I couldn't speak and didn't want to
frighten you.

I thought Sabina would scold me, but when I confessed it to
her she said only: Now it's over. And then, that night, I heard her
say to my father: You thought that child wouldn't love us because
he would always miss his parents: on the contrary.

Oh, when I'm grown up and go to Reggio Calabria, I want to
visit Messina, too. I was there a few times and I had a friend who
may remember me. Maybe, on the way, I'll stop in Naples, I'll put
all the pastries from here in my suitcase, you'll really like them. In
the meantime I'm putting in the envelope a little chocolate and
a photo in the snow, from that trip I told you about in the last
letter. My father came out better than in the other one, but my
mother is the same.

Now I have to go, tomorrow is the first day of school and I have to get my notebooks ready. I'm not going to study at home anymore, but will go to a real school. I'm excited.

Don't take too long to answer!

Nicola Crestani

# THE WORLD

*The first impression of the Card is therefore as if
the last Major Arcanum of the Tarot would suggest
a conception of the world as rhythmic movement
or dance of the female psyche, sustained by means
of the orchestral accompaniment of the four
primordial instincts, which gives the appearance
of a rainbow of colours and forms—or, in other
words, that the world is a work of art.*

Dear Rosalba,

It's six in the morning and I'm awake, and I want to take advantage of this moment of solitude to tell you about myself, how I've lived in these months. I'm sorry to have sent you only photos and greetings in the postscripts of Jutta's letters, but I couldn't write. I could justify it by saying that in the morning I was busy with school and in the afternoon I had to take care of Mimma, help Jutta in the kitchen, tidy up . . . And then the last weeks of pregnancy arrived and there was no room for anything else. But the excuses wouldn't be sufficient, the truth is that life besieged me all at once and the words were somewhere waiting.

But I always read your letters, and I glanced at the ones that

Jutta put in the envelope for you, envying the precision with which she kept you informed. I read her story of our Easter, but since she's modest she neglected to say she made a delicious *sciusceddu*, a dish so airy and light it seemed a cloud, a breath of eggs, ricotta, and meatballs that you will remember is typical of this city. It was wonderful. That day I, too, was a little resurrected, my nausea diminished and for the first time I tasted meat again. Even now, as I write, I think of Mother Fortunata's nasty looks when I refused it and she thought I was disdainful, but I was only pregnant.

I don't think Jutta told you about Theodore Roosevelt, who came to visit us in our misery. We were crushed in the crowd and only just managed to glimpse his back, a tiny distant black point, and that is the most we stole from the president's visit. Those who have relatives in America have already left, and those who remained have received donations from aunts and uncles and cousins celebrating their Italian origins with ostentatious charity. As you know, America has distributed photos of checks signed by generous philanthropists and tear-jerking stories of children called Giuseppe and Rosario, who beg in the alleys of New York for a dollar to send to their more unfortunate cousins in Italy. But no one has sent anything to us, I mean to Jutta, Elvira, and me. Messina has named a street for Roosevelt.

I realize I'm taking my time. It's pointless to linger on the summer, which was scorching and exhausting: Jutta already told you about the invasion of mice in the cabins, and how we exterminated them with sambuca leaves, and how in the heat we were so in need of everything. Luckily they gave pregnant women a double ration of water, otherwise I would have died of thirst, we would all have died of thirst. For me a parched throat is not a pleasant memory: maybe one day I'll tell you why.

So I'm getting there, I know what you want to know: yes, the baby we were expecting was born.

I gave birth on September 28th, at a quarter to twelve midnight. I felt the contractions in the morning, Mimma was at school, Elvira doing the shopping, and Jutta delivering clothes to her clients. She has a lot of work now (she's the most sought-after dressmaker in the city, she's too modest even to tell you that, so I assure you). I wasn't afraid because at the end of August a young midwife came to see me, younger than me, a girl with birth in her heart, who told me how to breathe, and who cheered me and calmed me simply by her presence. At lunchtime Elvira came home and I sent her to call the midwife, then Mimma came home, finally Jutta, and at night, as soon as the baby began to push, she came out on my bed, in the middle of us. Jutta cut the cord, we wanted that. I called the baby Cinzia, like the midwife. I didn't give her my mother's name, because I don't want to live looking at the past, I don't want any shadow to fall on my daughter, any destiny, her path must be free. Cinzia Cosentino belongs to no one, not even to me: She belongs to the world, to this sea, to this city that will take care of her. I want to hope that, with stubborn faith.

Remember when I told you that the eyes of a boy with long lashes came to see me in a dream? I thought they were my child's, that I would recognize them as soon as I brought her into the world. But they weren't Cinzia's, hers are pale, big and luminous: I told you she doesn't belong to the past, and since she was born those eyes have disappeared.

Dear Rosalba, I've written too much. My hand hurts, I'm not used to it anymore. Mimma has come over because it's late, time for school, and I have to make her snack, bread in milk with a thin slice of prosciutto, the way she likes. How much I want you to know her, why don't you come visit us at Christmas? In the new year she'll go to a school made of brick, not the cabin where for now another teacher is substituting. As for me, one thing is certain: as soon as possible I will enroll in the university, and I want to continue teaching. Elvira and Jutta encourage me and tell me that we can organize ourselves with schedules, daughters, and jobs.

Maybe in 1910 they'll give us real houses, but do you believe it? I've been hearing this story for months now. It doesn't matter. When it happens, we won't separate. We'll keep one house for ourselves and one for the children, for when they grow up. We have nothing but ourselves, but it's a lot.

I know, you want to know about Cinzia.

She's sleeping on my lap and she didn't wake up, even though this letter is full of emotions and she feels everything that happens to me. You must come in person to bring her your baptism gift, I don't want you to send it.

I kiss you, I expect you. Yours,
Barbara

# NOVEMBER 1919

A few days ago my daughter came home with a young man around twenty, twice as old as she is. Cinzia, I reminded her severely when she told me that a stranger had stopped her on the street and she had brought him to the steps of our house, Cinzia, I've told you a hundred times not to trust men.

Then a young man appeared. That is: a pair of eyes with long dark lashes. I was hurled to another time, another me. Silenced, I took a step back in the doorway.

"You don't recognize me, but I've never forgotten you," the boy said with a clear, slightly northern accent.

I moved aside to let him come in.

"How's Jutta?" my daughter asked.

I repeated the nurse's response: "Stable."

"This man said that you met during the earthquake," Cinzia continued, and she escaped to the kitchen to grab something to eat.

I asked the young man to sit on the best chair and I went to get a tray of walnut cookies bought just that morning. They're not as good as the ones Jutta makes, but I don't want to leave my daughter without sweets, these have already been difficult weeks.

"I know who you are," I said.

"I never knew if you had seen me or not," he answered, "but I couldn't be at peace until I had come looking for you to apologize."

The memories surfaced so clearly that I had to support myself on the table to be sure of not finding myself still on the *Morgana* but in my house, safe, on land.

"Apologize for what?" I asked.

"For having done nothing to protect you from a man whom today I would kill," he said. And then: "I didn't have this strength in my arms, I didn't even have a voice to yell, in fact it disappeared for a long time. You were the last night of my childhood."

"How did you find me?"

"It was a long search but not difficult," he said. "I came here to look for you, but first I stopped in Reggio, I wanted to see my house, which no longer exists, there's nothing, the people I knew are dead or have left, as I did. All except Madame." He paused. "Do you remember Madame? She returned to the Strait and opened a hotel for French tourists. You should visit her, she remembers you very well. I explained to her why I was here and I described you, and she recognized you, she told me she met you when you were pregnant."

I had never forgotten the Empress card, even though it had gradually slid into the depths of memory.

"She told me you were expecting a girl," he continued. "She had seen inside your belly, but she hadn't told you because you already seemed very frightened."

"I'd like to see her again," I said in a faint voice.

He continued, "So I took the ferry, it wasn't easy to get on a boat here, too much like that day, you know?"

I knew.

"I began looking up every girl born in the fall of 1909, then I went to a couple of schools, and, what can I say, I recognized her right away, she's like you, except for those very pale eyes."

"Not like me, luckily," I said quickly, because I didn't want my daughter to resemble anyone but herself.

We were silent, uncertain whether or not to name the sailor.

It was he who broke the silence.

"The city has changed," he said.

"They blew up everything," I answered, "churches, courtyards, colleges, the big hospital, the Palazzata . . ."

"What was still standing it was easier to sweep away," he resumed. "I read about it in the newspapers, this mania for reconstruction, and yet I wonder: why destroy where one could fix? What the earthquake took away from us, well, all right, but what humans have taken away from us I don't understand."

"And what the earthquake and dynamite didn't take the war took, and after that the Spanish flu," I added.

"I lost my mother in the pandemic," he said. "My true mother, I mean, that is, the one who adopted me."

"The families we're born into aren't always true families," I answered. "I lost a sister and a niece, and I'm fighting to save the second sister."

Thinking of Elvira and Mimma I became emotional, their loss was too near.

"I lost my father, too," I admitted, still feeling an intense remorse, because since the night of the earthquake I had never gone to Scaletta to look for him, to tell him that I was alive, and I had learned of his death by chance, months after it happened. And yet, in my heart, it wasn't I who had let him go but he who had let me die, replacing me with another child, that boy he would always have preferred to have. "We hadn't seen each other for a long time," I added.

The boy nodded. "The families we're born into aren't always true families," he repeated.

"I haven't asked your name."

"Nicola," he said. "Nicola Crestani. But when we met I was Nicola Fera."

Nicola stayed at our house all afternoon. He played with Cinzia, and he came back in the following days. Gradually he told me his story and I listened, one detail after another, and I saw those eyes with the long lashes, those phantom eyes become real.

The morning Nicola returned to Piedmont I went with him to the port. Before getting on the ferry he hesitated a moment.

"It's never pleasant to make this crossing," he said.

And I, with a bitter smile: "This time I'll stay here."

"You've always stayed here, right?"

"Let's say that the wish to get on a boat has passed."

From the parapet he continued to wave. I didn't leave the pier until his outline became a point and dissolved.

Now, as I recall the night in 1908 in my solitary psyche, that same sea of undertows and upheavals, that closed and volatile sea has absorbed the colors of twilight into its guts, and continues to release them little by little. Nothing can darken it. Its silver wakes are transformed into wine-colored crests, and I can recognize in certain orange flashes on the water the sunset's legacy. At night the sun is doubled: on the other side it has descended over the outline of Aspromonte, on this side its more violent rays have struck the majesty of Etna, subsiding only beyond Capo Peloro, beyond the turn of Mortelle, as the Tyrrhenian reaches toward the castle of Milazzo, facing the Aeolian islands. There the sun has descended into a sea that opens to the Mediterranean and is no longer the Strait.

Now, on the bridge of water that we once called the Bosporus of Italy, no wind disturbs my memories: the smallest boats rest on the shore, the fishing lights shine like fireflies, and both cities are extinguished.

It's dark, as it was then.

No voices on the sea, only a permanent and eternal silence.

No footsteps or whispers, tonight the dead make no sound. And yet, in the telling, they've arrived in the shadows to listen to their story, silent as those who know they still haven't had the right words. Many words have been expended, on 1908 and the time that followed: biased appropriations, ignoble omissions, arbitrary glorifications, truths assembled and disassembled according to what form to give the news. So we were called: news. Messina no longer exists, the newspapers repeated, while people speculated on its reconstruction. Reggio Calabria is finished, they insisted, and its inhabitants were replaced by others.

At the time I wanted to be a writer, like the writers of the novels that I thought would change my life. Then an apocalypse changed my life, and I had to invent for myself a career and a family, bring up a child. Survive.

A few months ago I went to the cemetery to find Elvira, Mimma, my grandmother. I had brought four bunches of flowers, the fourth was for Letteria Montoro, the author of the book I was reading on December 28th eleven years ago, now buried in the rubble of a Palazzata that no longer exists. Her tombstone was not rebuilt: Letteria Montoro was no longer anywhere, the guard confirmed it.

"We threw away the tombstones destroyed by the earthquake," he said.

"And the bodies?"

I got no answer.

Returning home, I opened the first drawer of the nightstand. Under my only silk scarf, next to Jutta's diamond and a pin that

Elvira left me, I touched the fragment of the tombstone I'd taken away with me when I went to find Letteria Montoro, right after the disaster. I took out the oval of her photograph and stared at it. I won't annihilate you, I whispered.

The next night, in the silence after I put my daughter to bed, I began to write what had happened to me during that year and what had happened to Nicola. I didn't want to lose anything of me or of him, of the events that I recalled clearly and those he had told me in our days together.

This is not the book I thought I'd write at twenty, but so rarely do we become what in our youth we think we are.

This novel of mine is no more than a reading among the shadows of history, where the lights are always out and the lives of people are crushed by false narratives. No more, but only now, with the last word, has the night stopped trembling.

# NOTES

Giovanni Pascoli, *Un poeta di lingua morta* (*Poet of a Dead Language*), 1898.

Marietta Salvo, "Ritornando nei luoghi" ("Returning to Places"), in *Vascello fantasma* (*Ghost Ship*), Perrone, Rome 2021.

Tarot citations: Anonymous, *Meditations on the Tarot: A Journey into Christian Hermeticism,* translated from the French by Robert Powell. [Originally published in French in 1980 by Aubier Montaigne.]

ABOUT THE AUTHOR

Nadia Terranova (Messina, 1978) is the author of *Gli anni al contrario* (Einaudi, 2015), *Casca il mondo* (Mondadori, 2016) and *Bruno, il bambino che imparò a volare* (Orecchio Acerbo, 2012). Her first novel translated into English, *Farewell Ghosts* (Seven Stories, 2020) was awarded the Premio Alassio Centolibri and was a finalist for the Premio Strega.

## ABOUT THE TRANSLATOR

Ann Goldstein is a former editor at *The New Yorker*. She has translated works by, among others, Primo Levi, Pier Paolo Pasolini, Elena Ferrante, Italo Calvino, and Alessandro Baricco, and is the editor of *The Complete Works of Primo Levi* in English. She has been the recipient of a Guggenheim fellowship and awards from the Italian Ministry of Foreign Affairs and the American Academy of Arts and Letters.